An Unforgiving Angel

Longarm took a threatening step toward his helpless prisoner but drew up short when the jail's front entrance burst open. Dressed in black from head to foot, a woman, nearly six feet tall and strikingly beautiful, stepped across the threshold and headed directly for One-Eyed Henry Hatchett, like someone who definitely meant business.

As though paralyzed by an event that bordered on the impossible to understand, Longarm watched, transfixed, as Hatchett twisted in the chair. The grim-faced female floated into the chained captive's limited view like a shadowy, vengeful angel. A wicked smile flitted across her flawless face.

"Oh, sweet merciful Jesus," Hatchett groaned. "You're supposed to be dead."

···TABOR EVANS···

LONGARM

AND THE GHOST
OF BLACK MESA

J

JOVE BOOKS, NEW YORK

THE BERKLEY PUBLISHING GROUP
Published by the Penguin Group
Penguin Group (USA) Inc.
375 Hudson Street, New York, New York 10014, USA

Penguin Group (Canada), 90 Eglinton Avenue East, Suite 700, Toronto, Ontario M4P 2Y3, Canada
(a division of Pearson Penguin Canada Inc.)
Penguin Books Ltd., 80 Strand, London WC2R 0RL, England
Penguin Group Ireland, 25 St. Stephen's Green, Dublin 2, Ireland (a division of Penguin Books Ltd.)
Penguin Group (Australia), 250 Camberwell Road, Camberwell, Victoria 3124, Australia
(a division of Pearson Australia Group Pty. Ltd.)
Penguin Books India Pvt. Ltd., 11 Community Centre, Panchsheel Park, New Delhi—110 017, India
Penguin Group (NZ), 67 Apollo Drive, Rosedale, North Shore 0745, Auckland, New Zealand
(a division of Pearson New Zealand Ltd.)
Penguin Books (South Africa) (Pty.) Ltd., 24 Sturdee Avenue, Rosebank, Johannesburg 2196,
South Africa

Penguin Books Ltd., Registered Offices: 80 Strand, London WC2R 0RL, England

This is a work of fiction. Names, characters, places, and incidents either are the product of the author's imagination or are used fictitiously, and any resemblance to actual persons, living or dead, business establishments, events, or locales is entirely coincidental.

LONGARM AND THE GHOST OF BLACK MESA

A Jove Book / published by arrangement with the author

PRINTING HISTORY
Jove edition / September 2007

Copyright © 2007 by The Berkley Publishing Group.
Cover illustration by Miro Sinovcic.

ISBN: 978-0-515-14352-2

JOVE®
Jove Books are published by The Berkley Publishing Group,
a division of Penguin Group (USA) Inc.,
375 Hudson Street, New York, New York 10014.
JOVE is a registered trademark of Penguin Group (USA) Inc.
The "J" design is a trademark belonging to Penguin Group (USA) Inc.

PRINTED IN THE UNITED STATES OF AMERICA

10 9 8 7 6 5 4 3 2 1

Chapter 1

Deputy Marshal Custis Long moved like a man on a mission, as he strode past Billy Vail's flabbergasted clerk and swept into the U.S. marshal's private office located in Denver's Federal Building. He stopped at the corner of Vail's desk, adjusted the Frontier model Colt pistol strapped cross-draw fashion over his left hip to a more comfortable spot for sitting, then slumped wordlessly into the well-worn morocco leather guest's chair directly across from his normally harried supervisor.

Legs scissored at the ankles, Longarm stretched his six-foot-four-inch frame to its maximum, snatched the snuff-colored Stetson from his head and dropped it onto the floor beside the rumpled, comfortable seat. He ran a finger under one side of his heavy moustache, then the other. Inquisitive, searching fingers darted to a blood-encrusted scalp, then tenderly explored their way through a matted shock of hair and split eyebrow. He scratched and fingered at several other sensitive spots on his head, then glanced around the overly warm and cluttered room, as though to check for anything new or different that might have appeared since his last visit ten days prior.

The severely chewed, square-cut nub of a nickel cheroot rolled from one corner of the bleary-eyed lawman's mouth

to the other. On its second journey, he snatched the gluti-
nous glob of tobacco from between chapped lips, and
stared at the thing for a moment. With a look of mild irritation, he flipped the mangled remnant into a polished brass
spittoon, strategically placed near the front corner of Billy
Vail's mahogany desk. A fresh smoke was immediately
drawn from an inside jacket pocket. He gave the new cheroot a quick back-and-forth under his nose and shoved the
rootlike stogie into his mouth without lighting it.

On the sly, Marshal Vail peeked up from the crumpled
page he'd randomly selected from the mountain of paper he
spent his days trying to wade through. A subtle, self-satisfied
smile made its way across his round, friendly, shaved pink
face, as he imperiously glanced back down at the official-
looking document clenched between stubby fingers. "You're
lookin' kinda like an empty shuck there, Custis. 'Pears like
somebody had their way with you, ole son."

Longarm squirmed deeper into the comforting leather
folds of his newly made nest. He cut an irritated, sharp-
eyed glance at the banjo-shaped clock ticking away the day
on the wall to his left, then rolled his gaze back to Billy
Vail.

Subtle evidence of West Virginia origins crept into the
lawman's soft, Southern speech when he said, "Gonna tell
you the God's truth, Billy. Right this very minute, feels like
I just single-handedly pumped a Southern Pacific Railroad
handcar all the way across the widest part of Texas and
back again. No doubt about it, I've got one axle a draggin'
in the dirt, that's for damned sure."

Vail tried to appear sympathetic. "You do look mighty
rough, Custis."

"Tell you the truth, Billy, my tongue's a hangin' out so
far it's a wonder I didn't leave three tracks just now, when I

came a barrelin' through your door. Probably have all the attributes of a winded dog. Know for damned sure, feels like I left most of my ass in pieces out on the trail somewheres."

Vail pitched the sheet of yellowed vellum onto the ever-widening foothills of the mountain of similar missives. The haystack-shaped mound slumped and dangled precariously over the edges of most of his entire desktop. Fighting evil seemed to take a lot of paper.

Vail's eyes crinkled, as he flicked a finger in Longarm's direction, then scratched at the corner of his mouth. "What the hell happened to your eye? Shit, I'd be willin' to bet you a shot of your Maryland rye that dimple hurts, don't it?"

Longarm rolled his head from one side to the other like an embarrassed hound dog caught red-pawed in the act of stealing food from its master's table. His neck hurt every time he turned his head, and he could hear the bones in his upper spine grind and pop. As if surprised at finding the wound, he fingered the scabbed-over, hand-stitched gash that raggedly zigzagged from his hairline down through the brow. "Hell, Billy, trust me when I say that you really don't want to hear about the particular dustup that resulted in this insignificant scratch."

"Oh that's where you're wrong, Custis. Yes, indeedy I can't wait to hear this tale. Come on, tell me what happened. You're gonna have to write a full report on the incident anyway. Might as well let the cat out of the bag right now. That way I won't be surprised by whatever in hell it is you're tryin' to avoid, when I read all about it."

Long shook his head and looked sneaky. "Aw, hell, surprise ain't got a damned thing to do with it. And, by God, I ain't tryin' to avoid nothin'." He shook his finger at Vail. "Like always, you're just a fishin' for a good laugh at my expense. That's what this all comes down to, ain't it?"

Vail showed upturned palms, as though begging for forgiveness, but a faintly sardonic smile danced across his lips, then almost instantly vanished. "Why, I had absolutely no idea a black eye, cut brow, and scratched-up face would involve *humor* at your expense, Longarm. No idea a'tall. Sent you out on a *plum* assignment, have absolutely no reason to find humor in the frightful vagaries of unforgiving providence that appear to have befallen you in the process of accomplishing that task."

Longarm rolled his eyes. Grim-faced, he threw Vail a peeved, guarded squint, then ran a tired hand from forehead to chin. "Plum assignment, huh? Did I hear you right? That's what you said, wasn't it? *Plum* assignment?"

"Plummest of the plum. All you had to do," Vail said, as he stood and proffered an open humidor of dollar cigars mined from one of his desk drawers, "was take a train up to Douglas, rent a horse, ride over to Lost Lance, arrest Limpin' Joe Cassidy, slap his sorry man-killin' ass in irons, and drag him on back to Denver for suitable trial and eventual execution."

Longarm slumped in the chair, as though he suddenly felt tired all the way to the bone. He gazed up at his boss through eyes that blinked like he could barely hold them open. But a rock-steady hand shot to Billy Vail's humidor and seized three of the expensive cigars before they could be snatched away. Two of the hand-rolled wonders, and the unlit cigar he'd barely managed to put a few teeth marks in, went into his jacket pocket, alongside half a dozen other freshly purchased nickel cheroots.

Using a sulfur match, he fired Vail's gift with a show of great flair and ceremony. A smiling Billy Vail got one of his own going and, in short order, a cloud of sweet-smelling, rum-laced tobacco smoke quickly filled the room

4

and drifted over both men like the warmth of a comforting fire on a cold night.

Longarm pushed himself up in the chair and waved his ash-tipped smoke at nothing in particular. "Here's how it went. Took the Union Pacific up to Douglas, just like you told me I should, Billy. Rented a horse. Stringy-muscled roan, but a right comfortable seat. Had me a nice easy ride to Lost Lance. Cool days, nip in the air at night. Fine trip. Tried my best to locate our contact, Marshal Turkey Creek Jack Williams, just soon as I set foot in town."

"Tried to locate him?"

Around the ax handle–sized cigar, which he'd jammed into one corner of his mouth, Longarm said, "Couldn't. Man had vanished from his pissant-sized, one-horse, one-dry-goods-store, one-saloon town like spit on a depot stove lid in February. Not a single trace of 'im, as I could find. And nobody in that end-of-the-road place knew nothin'. Not a damned thing. Dumbest bunch of hoople-headed, punkin' rollers I've ever encountered."

"So, you didn't find Limpin' Joe Cassidy?"

Longarm pulled the cigar from his mouth and shook it at Vail. "That's not what I said, Billy. Said I couldn't find Williams. Damned marshal's office was emptier'n last night's whiskey bottle, and none of them local yahoos, leastways any of those willin' to talk to me for more'n a heartbeat, would say much more'n good-bye and go to hell. People just didn't want to say nothin'. In addition to bein' dumber'n snubbin' posts, I do believe that was the scaredest bunch of folks I've ever seen."

Vail leaned on his elbow, the smoldering cigar held next to one ear. "You ever gonna get to the part about your eye, or am I gonna be sittin' here when I'm ninety years old, gummin' on this cigar with a toothless mouth?"

"Dammit, Billy, you had to ask. Wanted to hear the tale of how Custis Long, famous deputy marshal and man-hunter, got the whey beat outta him. So, you're gonna have to sit there and take the whole weasel—teeth, claws, hair, and all."

Vail raised his hands like a man being robbed in a ditch on the side of a remote New Mexico Territory stage route in the Tularosa Mountains. "You're right, Custis, absolutely right. I brought this pain on myself sure as hittin' my own thumb with a hammer. Go on and give me the rest of it."

Longarm nodded. "Damned right. All your fault, by God. Anyway, talked to the local banker. No help a'tall. Son of a bitch tried to loan me money. Then, when that didn't work, he tried to borrow some from me. Made more'n a passin' effort to speak with the owner of the only dry-goods store in town. Cross-eyed son of a bitch wouldn't even look at me. Come to think on it, maybe he couldn't look at me. Didn't have any trouble lookin' all around me though."

Vail smiled. "Gave up, huh?"

"Hell, no. Stopped a number of locals out on the street. Complete waste of time. Finally ambled over to a less-than-reputable-lookin' waterin' hole named the Wagon Wheel Saloon. Spotted Limpin' Joe soon as I poked my head over the batwing doors."

"Sounds like a real stroke of luck."

"Yeah. Suppose you could call it that. Ole Joe'd taken a seat in the far corner of the one-bartender joint and was a playin' poker with three other gents of equally dubious appearance. Had a dirty-legged, blond-haired gal draped around his spindly fuckin' neck. Single-minded woman kept tryin' to push one of her fully exposed, bullet-nippled breasts into his mouth."

6

Vail threw his head back, then shook it in disbelief. "Jesus."

"Oh, that ain't near the half of it. She kept the act up right to the point where I ambled over to the table and informed Limpin' Joe he was, by God, under arrest for usin' a double-bit ax to murder the hell out of Elroy Pottsy Morris down near Coal Creek last year. And, additionally, that he went a step further and chopped the poor man into four fairly equal, bloody parts. Pitched the warrant on the table and waited."

Billy Vail watched as Longarm's eyes slid closed. For several seconds it appeared as though his puffy-faced deputy had drifted off to sleep. "Well," the flustered marshal finally growled, "what the hell happened? You gonna tell me the rest of the tale, or do I have to get up, come over there like some cheap carnival seer, and figure it all out myself by feeling the bumps on your head, counting the corns on your feet, or maybe something else equally as stupid? Tale won't come oozin' out of your feet, crawl across the floor, seep into the bottoms of my boots, and make its way to my rusted-up thinker box."

Longarm's eyes flipped open like those of a kid who'd been caught red-handed with his grubby paw in the cookie jar. "Oh, yeah, well, like I was a sayin', loud and clear I informed Limpin' Joe he was under arrest. I had a hand on the butt of my Colt pistol. Figured the move would keep them other poker-playin' fellers at the table in their seats till I could escort Joe outside and slap the shackles on his butcherin' ass."

"Good idea."

"Be damned if that half-nekkid gal didn't jump off ole Joe's lap and go to pushin' her titties back inside her dress. And, well, that kinda distracted me for a second, you know.

Took my mind off the situation at hand, as it were. 'Fore I knew what was happenin', sneaky asshole on my right hopped up and whacked me across the side of my head with a half-full whiskey bottle."

"Ouch!"

"Course the damned bottle exploded. Knocked my hat off. Damn that evil bastard to an eternal, festerin' hell. Cut me pretty good. Came nigh on to coldcockin' my poor unsuspectin' ass into the next week, right then and there, Billy. I do not, to this very moment, know how I stayed conscious and standin' upright. Felt that rap on the noggin all the way to the soles of my boots."

"Jesus!" Vail whispered.

"Bet that bottle shattered into fifty jillion pieces. Glass and giggle juice shot around my head, all over hell and yonder. Flyin' fragments, liquor, and blood decorated the poor feller a playin' the pi-anner behind me. Last thing that bottle-swingin' son of a bitch ever did though, by God. Managed to get my pistol out, as I dropped to one knee. Cut loose and my first blast drilled a .45 slug into his ample gut, about two inches above his worthless dick. He yelped like a kicked dog, went to the floor a clutchin' at his blood-spurtin' guts. Put the second shot in that notch under his chin. That 'un came out the top of his rock-hard head, along with a handful of brains, and a purple gout of blood the size of an apple."

"Sweet merciful father."

"Right in the middle of everything that was happenin', Limpin' Joe pushed his chair away from the table, somehow got himself to drunken, wobbly feet, and went for an old cap'n ball Colt Dragoon he had shoved behind the waistband of his pants. Can't fathom how it happened, but somehow he got the damned pistol tangled up in his suspenders, thank God. So, just by absolute providential chance, I had time to shoot him in his only good foot, as I tried to scramble back onto my own feet."

"What the hell were the other fellers at the table doin'?"

"As it turned out, them other two were local boys, who didn't want nothin' to do with the possibility of gettin' shot to pieces by a blood-covered, highly pissed-off deputy marshal from Denver. They kicked their chairs over, turned tail, hit the door a runnin', and never looked back."

"You appear a bit more damaged than you've described, Custis."

"Well, Billy, that blond gal was another story altogether. Finally managed to get myself upright again 'bout the time she grabbed a second bottle and jumped on my back like a mama cougar a protectin' a pack of fuzzy kittens. Went to twirlin' around the room a tryin' to spin her off'n me. Knocked over every piece of cheap furniture in the whole damned place."

Vail turned his chair in an effort to make it appear that he wanted to look out the window. He stifled a chuckle at the image Longarm had conjured.

"God's truth, Billy, she beat me all over my head and shoulders with that damned bottle 'fore I could reach around and pull her off. Whole time I kept thinkin', why'n the hell is she so set on protectin' a worthless gob of spit like Limpin' Joe Cassidy? Finally decided that's just one of them unanswerable questions 'bout women that never becomes clear no matter how much a man puzzles over it. Damned women. Ain't ever gonna figure 'em out."

Vail threw his head back and hooted. Then he spun back around and said, "Can't believe that jug didn't shatter like glass in a freezing Montana norther. 'Specially when you have to consider she was whackin' on something as hard as your head. I've heard tell as how a man could bounce an anvil off Custis Long's head and not do even the slightest damage."

Longarm's eyes rolled toward heaven again, as though he felt the need to appeal to a higher authority for relief from those too ignorant to breathe. Then he grinned and said, "Well, fuck you, Marshal Billy Vail, and the three-legged, one-eyed horse you came to Denver on, by God. Gotta admit, though, it was probably the damndest thing I've had happen to me—lately. You'd a thought that piece of amber-colored glass that gal wielded was made out of fire-hardened steel. Bottle made this kinda *boinkin* sound ever time she bounced it off'n my brain pan." He gingerly touched spots on top of his head. "Still hurts, by God."

"Well, what happened to the girl?"

"Latched on to 'er by the front of what went for a dress, and shoved her away, once I got 'er off'n my back. But I'm damned if that crazed woman didn't snatch at the hem of her dress, and from behind a leather strap tied around her upper leg, she went and pulled a ten-inch-long coffin-handled Arkansas toothpick on me."

"Sweet Jesus, that's a helluva knife."

"Damned right. Anyhow, she come a screamin' back my direction like a runaway Denver and Rio Grande freight. Had that big ole pig sticker raised over her head like a blood-thirsty Comanche. Shit, near as I could tell, she meant business. Let her get close enough 'fore I dropped the butt of my pistol right betwixt her eyes. Gal went to ground like a burlap bag full of horse shoes. She was still a layin' there when I cuffed ole Limpin' Joe and dragged him out to his horse."

Billy Vail's chin dropped to his chest. He pounded on the pile of papers on his desk and laughed so hard, Long-arm thought the man might pass out.

10

"It ain't that damned funny, Billy. Just ain't no way, I'm aware of, to fathom the thinker mechanism of a woman. 'Specially a love-struck whore juiced up on laudanum, or some other such brain-alterin' shit. Who can know the mind or heart of such a person. Couldn't shoot her, for Christ's sake."

Between snorts, Vail huffed. "I agree, Custis. Couldn't shoot her. No way a'tall. Totally agree."

"Worse than all that, had to listen to Limpin' Joe bawl like a baby all the fuckin' way back to Denver. 'My foot hurts somethin' terrible, Marshal. Oh, God, my foot hurts.' By God, I told the whinin' sack of puss that was just too fuckin' bad, he'd just have to deal with it."

Vail pinched the bridge of his nose, then sucked in a lungful of air. "Beg to differ with you there, Custis. I have to admit now, that tale was funny. I can close my eyes and visualize the whole dance right now. Driftin' gun smoke, two men down. One dead. You spinnin' 'round the saloon with a bare-breasted demimonde attached to your neck, knockin' furniture all over the place. Her whackin' the be-jabbers out of you every chance she got with a whiskey bottle. Jesus, now you gotta admit, that's funny."

Longarm took another healthy puff off his cigar, then squirmed in his seat. "Well, I'm too tired to argue the point right now. Gimme a couple of days' rest and maybe I'll be able to put up a better case agin' the humor you've found in my recent predicament."

"Well, a couple of days is just about all the time you've got. Gonna have to hit the trail again soon as possible."

"Damnation, Billy, do I even get some time off 'fore I have to go out again? Just dropped ole Limpin' Joe off down in the lockup 'fore I came in here. Ain't even had no supper yet."

"Nope. Need you in Trinidad as quick as you can get there."

Longarm's head fell back against the chair. "Why?" he moaned. "I'm tired to the bone, Billy."

"City marshal, name of Mason Dobbs, down that way's pretty sure he's seen the one-and-only Quincy 'the Spook' Lomax hauntin' places in and around his town."

Mere mention of Spook Lomax's vile name caused both men to feel as though an evil spirit, covered from head to toe in the detritus of a gory past, had stealthily invaded the comforting camaraderie of Billy Vail's office. Wafting on a barely perceptible puff of air through each man's memory of the past, the white-faced phantom smelled of spent gunpowder, sulfur, blood, and violent death—all the things men who labored under the weight of a badge hated with a passion.

Chapter 2

Longarm's head snapped away from the conversation. He looked like a man who'd just been slapped with an open palm made of red-hot, fresh-forged iron. A wave of pent-up, bitter-tasting bile, anger, and disgust swept through his entire being. His weathered neck reddened, and he jerked his tightly buttoned shirt collar open for relief from the sudden upsurge of heat flowing toward his ears. All of a sudden he felt discomfort from the soles of his feet to the roots of his hair. A murderous fury, generated from the intensity of long-suppressed feelings, swept through blood that bubbled, then instantaneously went to a lethal, skin-singeing, man-killing boil.

The most primitive of instincts took over his entire being. Displaying an exterior calm that belied his inner turmoil, Longarm slipped a hand over the butt of the heavy pistol lying across his belly. He shot a wary, probing glance around the room and into every shadowed corner.

To Billy Vail, it appeared that his droopy-eyed deputy was reacting as though Spook Lomax would somehow inexplicably pop from behind a bookcase, or emerge from the carpet like a long-drowned swimmer rising from the depths of a cold, unfeeling river.

The unnerving images of pooled sticky gore, rendered

13

bone, mangled flesh, and the breathy departure of life, as it seeped from Lydia Jefferys's cold, gray death-mask of a face, flashed up like a fading tintype on the backs of Longarm's tired eyes.

Like sharpened knives, the lawman's previously stifled recollections crackled across the inside of his skull, sliced a new set of jagged wounds on his brain, then headed for his heart. Razor-sharp visions of horrific death left fresh and painful scars atop those already in residence—ancient mutilations so painful he seldom allowed conscious thought of them to have a spot in the forefront of his crowded memory.

Longarm came nigh crushing his boss's expensive cigar between tense, knotted fingers, when he shook it in Billy Vail's face and snarled, "Spook Lomax? You mean Satan's younger brother come to life right here on earth? Quincy the Terrible?"

"The very one, Custis. The very one."

"Well, by God, I hope you instructed Marshal Mason the-well-known-dumb-ass Dobbs to arrest that sorry, theivin', woman-killin', child-murderin' bastard's no-account self, and right goddamned quick? Better yet, Billy, hope you told Dobbs to kill the motherless, soulless, walkin' stack of rottin' shit, at his earliest possible opportunity. But knowin' Dobbs the way I do, it would take harshly worded, direct orders screamed right in his face to get the man off his lazy, cowardly, calloused ass long enough to do much of anything."

Vail's sympathetic gaze met Longarm's defiant glare and held it for a second. He quickly broke the fleeting connection, then cast nervous looks of his own around the room. "I sent a telegram yesterday with something very much akin to those exact sentiments, Custis. As you might imagine, Marshal Dobbs wired back and informed me that his responsibilities, as outlined by Trinidad's recently adopted city charter, did not include confronting vicious criminals of Spook Lomax's well-documented, murderous inclinations. Unless said criminals wantonly violated local law, or were the source of violent behavior while in his jurisdiction."

"Well, what exactly, in the blue-eyed hell, does he think his fuckin' responsibilities *do* include, Billy?"

A rueful grin carved its way across Marshal Vail's open, friendly face. "Near as I'm able to determine, the illustrious Trinidad city marshal presently feels that he is accountable for little more than keeping the town's wagon-rutted, dirt streets free of pig wallows, dead dogs, unconscious drunks, aggressive whores out to do the deed while leaned up against any horse available, and, of course, mountains of horse and cow shit."

"And that's it? That's the sum total of what Dobbs feels is his responsibility to the community, the county, and the state? Keepin' the streets clean?"

"Well, he also harbors some belief in a degree of personal accountability for arresting those who appear publicly intoxicated, seeing to the safety and welfare of local citizens, as deemed necessary, and any other tasks as assigned, or requested, by the city fathers. According to Marshal Dobbs's interpretation of those duties, none of them include going after a killer like Quincy 'the Spook' Lomax, just because some federal asshole from Denver wants him to do it. 'Sides, he says he can't actually find ole Spook, but he's pretty sure the man is in town."

"You're pullin' my fuckin' leg, right, Billy? The poor moron can't find a six-and-a-half-foot-tall albino with eyes that look like they belong on a big white rabbit? God Almighty, ole Spook might well be the palest-complected man walking God's blue-skied, green-grassed earth at this very moment. Son of a bitch looks like he was born dipped in a bucket of whitewash."

"All I can tell you is what Dobbs said in his various telegrams."

"Dobbs's attitude on this matter ain't nothin' more'n a wagonload of horse shit, if I ever heard it, Billy. Man's just afraid to do his duty. That is, by God, all the cowardly bucket of stink amounts to."

Longarm violently puffed on the cigar a time or two more, scratched his head, then added, " 'Course I can't, in good conscience, blame him too much, when it comes to the Spook. Already put at least two bullets in that ghostly son of a bitch myself. Either one of 'em would've killed most men."

Vail nodded. "Believe me, I hear and understand."

"Not sure you do, Billy. Scary bastard just laughed at me. Can you believe it? Laughed at me like somethin' insane. Like a creature not of this world. Then he saddled up and rode off like nothing had happened. Can still see his duster flappin' in the wind like the grave clothes taken from a recently buried corpse." Longarm shook all over as though in the throes of the ague. "Shit. Gives me the shiverin' willies and makes my scrotum draw up like the top skin on a regimental drumhead just talkin' 'bout 'im."

Vail took on a thoughtful countenance and, using a single finger, traced a poorly formed circle through the layer of accumulated dust in the only bare spot atop his desk. "Any chance you might have missed him, Custis? Is it possible them two shots you threw at him just whizzed on by?"

Longarm snapped erect and sliced through the overly warm, dense office air with his smoking cigar. "Hell, no, I didn't miss 'im. You know me, Billy. If I say I shot a man,

16

then by God I shot him. And I'm tellin' you here and now, I've stood toe to toe with that ghoulish apparition that walks like a man, and I put two chunks of burnin'-hot lead in his flour-white ass. The creepy son of a bitch should've been dead twice over. Yessir. Should've been deader'n Stonewall Jackson, by God."

"Was that before or after you tracked him all the way to the Salt River and found those bodies in the log cabin?"

Longarm slumped back in the chair like a man who'd just had all the air sucked out of his lungs. His head lolled back and forth as though the bones in a painfully sore neck had, without any forewarning, gone completely soft. "Just didn't get there fast enough. All there is to it. Damn near ran into ole Spook as he was a comin' outta the front door of that place."

The U.S. marshal shook his head. "Amazing."

A pained look from Longarm welded Vail to his seat. "Swear 'fore Jesus, Billy, at a distance of little more than arm's length, I plugged the man twice. Saw his duster and the shirt beneath jump both times with the impact. Eerie, dead-eyed, cocksucker smiled at me—smiled like we were long-lost friends, family, or somethin'. Then he turned and left me with that crazed laughter ringing in my ears. I came near fallin' down dead from the shock right on the spot."

"Amazing."

"For about a second, I was so stunned by what happened, just naturally got stupider'n a snubbin' post. Then he sent a blue whistler across my noggin that knocked me damned near senseless. Went down like a felled oak. Nowadays I try not to think on the event unless I have to. But if I think on it, I can see him clear as day a sweepin' off that cabin's little covered porch. A walkin' phantom trailin' all its grave-contaminated raiments behind him like a

17

molasses-drenched flag flutterin' in the stench-dripping breezes of Beelzebub's favorite wallerin' spot in hell."

Vail's eyes rolled back and his chin dipped to his chest. He pinched the bridge of his nose, then rubbed aching temples. "Can't begin to imagine the inside of that blood-saturated house, even after reading your full report on the matter, Custis. Just can't imagine it. Seen plenty myself, but I'm not sure how I would have handled the situation."

Longarm sounded distant, as though speaking from the bottom of a grave, when he said, "The reality was far worse than my paltry ability to provide a fully realized, written description, Billy."

Vail shook his head, "Hell, I got sick from simply seeing such words on paper. Couldn't even bring myself to show your gruesome account of the event to Preston Jefferys. Poor man was so distraught over the little I did tell him about the entire vicious incident. In the end, though, an abbreviated rendition of the events as you saw them seemed to satisfy him of the finality of the whole ordeal. Know he felt a great debt of gratitude to you, Custis, for making such a mighty effort on behalf of his poor wife and young son."

Longarm appeared to sag into the cushions of the over-stuffed leather chair, but he kept his hand on the pistol butt. The stoked flames from a deep and abiding hatred still flared behind his normally gracious and affable blue-gray eyes. In refreshed memory, the skeletal countenance of Spook Lomax mockingly stared back at him from the smoky, muddled past and pointed with a bony, blood-tipped finger to the dreadful sights that awaited inside the cabin of horrors on the Salt River.

Unsettling visions of his tortured crawl through the spattered remains of young Timothy Jefferys to a spot be-side the still gasping body of the boy's recently butchered mother had plagued Longarm's nighttime reveries ever since that terrible day. At strange and unexpected times, just the right amount of Maryland rye had the power to conjure the face of Lydia Jefferys from beyond the grave he'd dug for her with his own bare hands.

Longarm squeezed his eyes shut. He sadly shook his head, as if in a futile effort to eject the wicked recollections from his tortured mind. His efforts didn't altogether work. No one deserved to die the way Lydia Jefferys had, he thought. Not even the most malevolent two-legged creature deserved to be chopped into pieces with an ax while living. He still found it hard to believe the woman managed to survive and breathe her final words on earth into his waiting ear.

In a bleak, seldom-visited corner deep inside his soul, he knew the only way to purge himself of the whole blood-soaked affair was to find Spook Lomax, then erase the evil son of a bitch from the world of the living by whatever means necessary.

Vail watched as his deputy struggled with but one of a host of demons swarming over his brutal past and chipping away at the foundations of his amiable nature. "Suppose I could send someone else, if you'd prefer to take a pass on this one," he offered.

Longarm's eyes snapped open like paper window shades in a Hell's Half Acre whorehouse. A two-inch piece of ash broke off the cigar and dropped to the floor, as he shook it at Vail again. "Damned if you will, Billy. I swore a solemn oath to that poor dyin' woman that I'd find Spook Lomax and kill him graveyard dead. By God, I intend on doin' it. If someone saw him down in Trinidad, I'll be on my way there as soon as I can get some rest. Maybe even tomorrow afternoon, if I'm rested up enough."

Vail stood and started a slow amble toward the door. Longarm took the hint and followed. In the marshal's outer office, Vail stopped and placed a sympathetic hand on his deputy's shoulder. From an inside coat pocket he pulled a manila envelope. "Everything you need is in here, Custis—money, travel arrangements, letters of introduction, and such. Henry's been working on it ever since we got the message from Dobbs. Anything else you might require at some future time, just send word."

As Longarm fingered the envelope, Vail leaned closer and whispered, "I know you're aware that Mrs. Jefferys and her son weren't Spook Lomax's only victims, when you last went out after him. Near as I can tell from newspaper accounts and reports from law enforcement officials over five neighboring states, he murdered at least seventeen people during that homicidal rip—maybe more."

"Hell, I know that, Billy. Saw his bloody handiwork up close, firsthand."

"Most of the dead were just innocent folk trying their best to get by, live their lives, make a living—storekeepers, bankers, ranchers, women, and, sometimes, even children. Want you to listen carefully to what I'm about to say, Custis. This is just between you and me."

Longarm's eyes narrowed, as he tilted his head more in Vail's direction. "I'm listenin'."

"I'll swear you're lying if you ever tell anyone I said this, but as far as I'm concerned you needn't make any real effort to bring Spook Lomax back for trial. Given any reason whatsoever, first chance you get, do the world a gigantic favor and kill the man. Kill him before he has a chance to populate our graveyards with the corpses of any more innocents."

Longarm shook his friend's hand. A faint smile spread over his face as he said, "Trust me, Billy. From the moment you told me he was a hauntin' the area again, I never entertained the slightest intention of bringing him back alive. He's dead already—he just don't know it yet."

Chapter 3

Sugar-scented, ice-tinged breezes swept down on Denver directly from the snow-covered peaks of the Rocky Mountain's front range some fifteen miles away as Longarm pushed through the doors of the Denver Federal Building and headed toward his spartan room located near Cherry Creek.

The change in temperature from Billy Vail's overheated office felt good on Longarm's still flushed face. His long-legged, purposeful stride down the sandstone sidewalk was broken only once at the corner of Cherokee and Colfax. Still agitated all the way down to his boots, he stopped for a moment and disposed of the stub of Billy's rum-soaked gift, lit a fresh cheroot, puffed it to life, then continued on his way in a semi-trot.

Barely half an hour later, his ears still burning with the single-minded prospect of avenging the Jefferys' brutal murders, Longarm kneeled on the floor of his shabby digs. From beneath the lumpy-mattressed, run-down brass bedstead, he dragged a heavy canvas satchel, held closed with thick leather straps and tarnished, pot-metal buckles. He jerked the moldy leather bindings loose and pried the massive case open. A pair of well-kept, walnut-gripped pistols was extracted from the bag—along with a hand-tooled holster for each weapon. The guns were already cleaned, oiled, and ready for deadly action.

Longarm sat spraddle-legged on a worn wine-colored oriental rug. With a practiced eye, he examined the first piece—a short-barreled .45-caliber model 1873 Colt with the sight filed off and a very touchy trigger tuned especially for gunplay. The revolver was, beyond any doubt, a professional man-killer's weapon. He slid the shooter and holster onto a thick cartridge belt so it would hang at his back, the grip easily accessible from the right.

The second pistol was a cavalry model of the same make of weapon, with a seven-and-a-half-inch barrel—a better than average sidearm, especially when firing at a distant target from horseback. He half-cocked the revolver, flipped the loading gate open, and set the glistening cylinder to spinning. Everything appeared in order, and the cavalry Colt was settled on the right side of the tooled belt so it came to rest on his hip, butt first, in the contrary fashion of famed gunfighters like Wild Bill Hickok and Long Hair Jim Courtright.

Along with the Frontier model Colt that Longarm carried mounted on his left hip in cross-draw fashion, the newly added weapons and fully loaded cartridge belt weighed nigh on thirteen pounds. In an effort to better distribute the weight around his waist and make the load easier and a bit more comfortable to carry, he fastened a set of thick suspenders that attached to special brass buttons stitched onto the back side of the leather belt. The braces served to spread and lighten the burden of heavy iron and would, he felt, make the entire rig considerably easier to deal with over long periods of time.

Next, the bag yielded a sawed-off, double-barreled, .12-gauge shotgun. At some point in the past, he'd removed the big popper's wooden stock down to the pistol grip and added a stout leather sling mounted on metal swivels so the heavy blaster could be draped over a man's shoulders. Given everything that had been removed from the original two-shot boomer, the weapon measured out at just barely over two feet in length, was as easy to use as eatin' Grandma's apple pie, and lethal in the extreme when brought to bear in cramped spaces.

With a resounding *snap*, Longram broke the shotgun open and blew into the empty chambers before dropping a shiny brass shell of heavy-gauge shot into each chamber. He snapped the weapon shut, wiped it with an oily piece of rag, and laid it across the growing pile of armaments that littered the floor.

"Just can't be too careful or too well armed when it comes to men like Lomax," he mumbled to himself.

All of a sudden, Longarm noticed a barely discernible catlike scratching from outside his room's door. The weary lawman slapped the canvas bag closed and quickly pushed it back under the bed. He snatched up all the guns and laid them in a chair beside his ramshackle washstand. He knew, without even thinking about it, which stray was making the noise at his door, but remained cautious nonetheless. Barefoot, dressed in nothing but his balbriggans, and with the Frontier model Colt in hand, he silently slipped to the unsecured portal and snatched it open.

An ebony-haired, hazel-eyed beauty seductively leaned against his door frame. Her bright, near perfect smile flashed across a face that glowed from exposure to the refreshing wind. Raised hands trembled in feigned terror. She pressed her arms against the sides of a spectacular pair of breasts in what Longarm instantly recognized as a deliberately provocative action—a move that appeared to enlarge the already sizable, upturned, perky globes, and at the same time boldly pushed them forward and out for better viewing, admiration, and access.

"Why, Custis, darlin'," the stunning girl cooed, "you ain't really gonna shoot a poor little ole, unarmed, totally defenseless gal like me, are you?"

Longarm frowned, poked his head into the chilly hallway, then suspiciously glanced down the nippy passage in both directions. He grabbed the cat-eyed beauty by the arm, pulled her inside, then silently eased the door closed and set the latch.

He watched with more than a passing interest as his unannounced guest, trailing the heavy scents of gardenias and randy woman, flounced to the edge of the bed, then turned, and flopped onto the mattress. She made quite a show of throwing off an ankle-length fur coat, drew one knee up against an ample, near totally exposed bosom, then went into something akin to an incurable, puffy-lipped pout.

He let the hammer down on the pistol and shoved the gun back into its holster. "What're you doin' here, Geneva? I coulda sworn you were on the way back to that fancy finishin' school for young ladies in Boston."

The girl leaned against a pile of pillows in a way that ensured Longarm could see her exposed, diamond-hard nipples. "That's not till next week, darlin'. Got bored sittin' at home all alone. Felt like I needed a bit of that kind of *special attention* only you can provide 'fore I headed back East."

Longarm allowed himself a knowing grin. "Well, God help the young men of Boston when you get there."

"Indeed," the girl oozed, then licked her crimson lips. "Maybe even all those on the whole East Coast."

Longarm pitched the heavy pistol belt onto the chair with the guns. Hands on his hips, he turned his full attention on the girl and snapped, "Not sure I have time for this kinda dance tonight, Gen. I'm so tired right now, feels like I could sleep for a solid week layin' buck-assed nekkid on a brand-new roll of barbed wire fence during a west Texas thunderstorm."

The girl shook coal-colored hair that fell to her shoulders in a sea of shining, light-flecked ringlets. She grasped the hem of her dress and flipped it at him. The action revealed far more than most women would have dared. "Well, Daddy had to go up to Casper, and I've just been bored stupid for almost a week now. Took Eli with him, too. No Daddy at home. No young, inexperienced suitors left around to entertain me. You know how easy it is for me to get to feelin' ignored, Custis. And you, of all people, should know what I like to do when I find myself in such a state."

He pointed at the ever-creeping hem of her dress, about the time it arrived at the spot that ensured he could see the fleshy, steaming treasures awaiting beneath. "Forgot to put any underthings on before you came over as well, didn't you?"

A radiant, ruby-lipped grin played across the impish girl's flawless face. "Figured since I was comin' to see you and knew exactly what we'd likely be doin', I wouldn't be needin' no underthings. 'Sides, makes me hotter'n a burnin' cowboy boot anytime I'm right on the edge of bein' nekkid in public." She ran the tip of an insistent finger around a nipple that peeked out at him from behind the gauzy blouse she'd obviously made not the slightest effort to lace up.

Longarm strode to the bedside with every intention of swatting Geneva Blackstock's drop-dead gorgeous behind, then putting her back out in the hall, and on her way to a much tonier part of town. But as soon as he was close enough, her hand shot up to his crotch, quickly found his semi-rigid cock behind the thin cotton material of his balbriggans, and began the kind of massage any real man would have found impossible to resist. Halfheartedly, he pushed the talented hand away. She flashed another perfect white-toothed smile and grabbed for his now stiffer-than-a-fire-poker prong again.

"Come on, Custis. Let's you and me play some. You know how I like to come over when you're in town and play. You can be Doctor Long. I'll be your seriously *needy* patient. You can give me one of your special treatments. The kind *needy girls* all over Denver like me are joyously familiar with. Relieve me of some of my vapors."

He cupped her beautiful face in his hands. "You are one bad, bad girl, Geneva. Knew the night I spotted you at that Frenchified eatin' joint up near the capitol that you were gonna be a problem. Could tell all the way across that room you were smolderin' like a forest fire just a waitin' to burst out into an inferno. Walkin', talkin', struttin' dynamite. Damnation, I shoulda stayed the hell away from you, girl. But if there's two things I do know for sure, you're beautiful, and I'm weak."

She leaned forward and rubbed her face against his crotch, then went back to her massage. "Why, that was two years ago, Custis, and I ain't been no *real* trouble so far, have I? I only bother you when that special itch just gets so bad it has to be scratched."

Longarm's head fell back as her ardent ministrations resumed and got more enthusiastic. In spite of his very real irritation at being taken away from what he considered important travel preparations, a leering grin etched its way across his deeply tanned face. "No, Geneva, you haven't been any *real* trouble thus far. And I suppose there's worse things than scratchin' your particular itch. Yes, Jesus, there's a helluva lot worse things," he mumbled toward the ceiling.

She stopped trying to suck him through his balbriggans for a second, but continued with a well-practiced rubbing of his rigid prong. "Well, of course there are, darlin'. Why, I'm just a little ole former Mississippi gal lookin' for some fun, whose daddy struck it rich three different times in a nasty, stinky, little place named Leadville. Then went and bought up every piece of cattle-grazing land he could get his greedy hands on in Colorado and Wyoming, which made him rich ten times over again."

"Know you're rich, Geneva. Don't have to remind me none."

"Well, that's why Eli's with Daddy right now. The boy's family has all the money in the world, but he's obviously after mine as well, or at the very least, what he perceives as what'll be mine when Daddy buys that big ole cattle ranch in the sky. Guess when Daddy finally cashes in his chips, I'll just be the living embodiment of the wildly beautiful, jaded, rich girl. Whadda you think, Custis? Think I'm beautiful and jaded?"

"Girl, I think you hit that nail right on the head. And in so doing you've graphically pointed out the danger-filled nub of our problem. Yes, for damned sure, your daddy is fantastically rich. He's also a dangerous old coot. And I'd be willin' to bet he's gonna want my *cojones* mounted on a

29

sharp stick and flame roasted over an open fire when, or if, he ever finds out you've been sneakin' over here to *play with Dr. Long*, while he's out of town with your favorite suitor checkin' on his Wyomin' cattle holdin's."

With no further discussion, she yanked at the waist tie of his underwear until they lay in a heap around his ankles. Anxious fingers trembled as she caressed his ax-handle-stiff rod again. Her twinkling hazel eyes flared open. "Heavens. Sight of this beautiful thing just sets my lips to rejoicin'. This is what I've wanted, and been thinkin' 'bout all day long. Makes me tingly all over when I'm suckin' on it," she said, then took him into her hot mouth.

Between noisy sucks and licks, she held the blood-engorged tip of his unbending manhood against her lower lip and moaned. "Good God, Custis, this has got to be the closest thing to suckin' on a real, live railroad spike I'm ever gonna have the opportunity to experience in this life."

Longarm glanced down. He noticed that Geneva's blouse had somehow miraculously disappeared, and he watched as the flushed, superheated girl caressed one of her own breasts, then vigorously rolled the nipple between a thumb and finger. When he gently pulled her to her feet, then pushed the fiery female onto her back, shapely legs sprang apart and revealed a coal-black, silken thatch that covered the luscious, glistening, velvety prize at the center of her being.

She pulled her own knees down against two-fisted breasts tipped with dark, brownish-pink areolas the size of twenty-dollar gold pieces. Longarm knew that the girl had the kind of nipples that, when properly coaxed with a talented tongue, would harden, stand to rigid attention, and grow to impressive lengths. He'd even seen her lick those beauties herself when in the throes of unfettered sexual rapture.

As he crawled between Geneva's shapely legs, she ran an inflamed hand as far down as she could stretch, then slid stiletto-sharp fingernails from the base of his balls to the tip of his throbbing cock. "Come on, Custis," she whimpered, "do the deed till I'm so weak I can't even lick my upper lip. Wear me down to a sweaty frazzle."

With a burst of authority, he plunged forward and pressed himself deep into the waiting heat and fire. Breathlessly, she threw one arm around his neck and whispered into his ear, "Make some magic with that big, wonderful wand of yours, darlin'. Do it in a way I'll still remember fondly, even when I'm so old people will think I've been around since the Dead Sea was just feelin' a bit on the puny side."

Muscular legs snapped together around Longarm's waist like a powerful, fleshy vise. Any modesty Geneva Blackstock might have ever possessed vanished by the time he'd made his fourth or fifth depth-probing stroke. "Oh, Jesus," she squealed, "I can't believe it! I've already come—twice! More! More! Harder! Make me come again! Oh yes, that's it!"

Longarm bounced the girl from one side of his well-used bed to the other, then from one end to the other. The brass frame hopped, popped, and groaned like a living thing, then rattled and squealed its metallic objections at being so roughly abused. Anyone passing in the hallway would have sworn the sounds emanating from the room had the power to jar apples out of a tree.

Fifteen or twenty minutes into their bawdy, noisy tussle, they rolled onto the floor atop a patchwork quilt and sev-

31

eral pillows dragged from the bed as they fell. Geneva brought her legs up as high as she could, locked her ankles behind her muscular lover's head, and tried to match his pistonlike thrusts with an equally powerful upward pump of her impressively built, shapely buttocks.

She threw sweat-slick arms around his neck and pulled herself up till her mouth was against his ear again. A glistening sheen of sweat bathed their bodies when she whispered, "My God, you're the only man yet who's actually found the bottom of me!" Wild-eyed as a spooked colt, she abruptly pushed back into their improvised pallet and redoubled frantic efforts to equal every plunge he made into her creamy, volcanic depths.

Smiling, Longarm gazed down at the girl's flushed upper body. One of her hands had snaked its way down between the two of them once more and frenetically rubbed the frothy, magic spot hidden in the glorious folds of a pussy that rippled and gushed its satisfaction with their combined efforts.

The other hand clutched at a perfect breast, firm from her own energetic caresses. A stiff nipple protruded from between Geneva's clutching fingers like a man's thumb. To Longarm's smiling wonder, the exuberant girl craned her neck forward, pushed upward, licked the nipple, then sucked it. Inspired by such blatantly carnal feats, he upped his bucking, lunging exertions once more, and pounded into her with renewed force and vigor.

A few minutes later, his back and arm muscles turned into something akin to steel cables. Rivers of salty sweat dripped onto Geneva Blackstock's board-flat belly and ran into a tiny lake that formed inside her indented navel. She frantically licked from one nipple to the other, and urged him on between ardent slurps by yelping, "Come on! Do it!

Come on, baby! Come inside me!" His iron-willed resolve to hold back crumbled.

All of a sudden, he reached up, grabbed the bedstead's lower frame with both hands, then bored into her with such enthusiasm the entire room seemed to shake as though being ripped apart by a springtime tornado. Geneva clamped her legs together even tighter and, using all the leverage at her disposal, raised him into the air like a gigantic rag doll. They held the pose while he emptied himself into the depths of her lava-hot, receptive body. He spewed himself into her like a Gatling gun being cranked at top speed.

Spent, Longarm's fatigue finally caught up with him, and he rolled to one side. Geneva grabbed at his still-pumping dingus but he pushed her hand away. "Enough, girl. Enough. Christ Almighty. Gimme a break. Gotta let me rest for at least a minute or two. Maybe more. Have a tough day ahead of me tomorrow."

Geneva hopped up, rummaged in the piles of their clothing until she came up with one of his cheroots, then lit it. She blew smoke toward the ceiling, fluffed up a pillow she retrieved from the floor, then flopped back down beside him. "Mind if I stay the night, Custis, darlin'? We could do that again three or four more times, couldn't we?"

"Well, if you'll leave me alone long enough for some much needed sleep, maybe you can stay a little longer. Feel like we've been gambling with fire for a spell now, Gen. We keep up this kind a pace and you're gonna end up *with child* sooner or later."

Geneva Blackstock threw her head back against her pillow and snorted out a stifled laugh behind her hand. "You needn't concern yourself, Custis," she finally said. "Prospect of such an event is not even remotely possible."

He leaned over and took the smoking cheroot from between her fingers. "How so?"

She rolled against him, her chin resting against his shoulder. "Childhood accident. I can't have children. Ever. So you don't have to trouble yourself with such concerns." Her hand found him again and began the sensuous massage all over again. "And besides, while I know how you Southern boys are about such things, I wouldn't marry you if I could get pregnant."

"Never said nothin' 'bout gettin' married, did I?"

"Well, that's what you were implyin'."

"Wasn't implyin' anythin'," Custis said. "Just makin' an observation's all."

Geneva licked her way down to a nipple and sucked on it for a second, then said, "Soon's my schoolin's over, I'm gonna marry Eli for sure. His family has money. Lots and lots of money. You're an itinerant lawman who's rarely at home and who barely makes enough to live on. Not much to recommend a man for marriage."

Longarm dropped the now dead cheroot into a damp-bottomed glass he retrieved from the table beside the bed, turned to the energetic girl, and propped himself up on one elbow. "Guess we'd best get as much done as possible 'fore the big event then. I admit to having some personally held ethical problems when it comes to doin' the big wiggle with married ladies, Geneva. Just never cared much for it like that."

She stared into his eyes for a moment, caressed his cheek, then said, "We started out as friends, among other things, Custis. And we're still friends. I fully expect that won't change, no matter what else happens in this life. So you might as well get used to the whole idea right now. Way I've got it all planned out, you'll be seeing plenty of me for as long as I can find you. So, our *relationship*, how-ever you choose to define it, isn't going to change. Not very much, anyway. You're still gonna be doing this with me for the foreseeable future, because that's the way I want it. Understood?"

Longarm flashed a quick grin, then crawled on top of the giggling girl for a second fiery helping of the fleshy pleasures spreading beneath him.

Chapter 4

Way too early the following morning, an obliging Denver & Rio Grande conductor helped Longarm with all his possibles, weapons, and equipment, as he clambered aboard the passenger coach of the chuffing, steam-belching train.

"You'll be more comfortable back in this spot against the bulkhead, Marshal Long," the genial conductor offered. "We'll just throw your belongin's in one seat. That-a-way you can stretch out in the other and sleep—if'n you've a mind to, that is. I can wake you anytime you'd like, or just let you nap at your leisure."

Longarm shook the man's hand, thanked him for his kind attention, then dropped into the rigid, uncomfortable benchlike affair that passed for a seat. He pulled the snuff-colored Stetson down over his face, and immediately fell into a much welcomed slumber. The previous evening's rambunctious, cavorting gyrations with Geneva Blackstock had finally screeched to a halt around three that morning, and he felt like a man who'd been whipped all the way to the Rockies and back with a knotted rope.

Some hours later, the bleary-eyed lawman snapped awake as the Baldwin engine ground to a halt at the Pueblo rail station. He roused himself long enough to stretch like a waking mountain lion, then briefly stepped onto the passenger- and freight-loading platform.

He purchased half a dozen spicy meat-filled tortillas from a Mexican kid who sold the tasty morsels out of a wooden box that dangled from a leather strap around his skinny brown neck. Once the train started moving again, Longarm stretched out in his seat and devoured all the tortillas like a ravenous animal.

Upon arrival in Trinidad, he hired a hack near the D&RG station house. One wheel of the flatbed, spring wagon screeched like it needed a serious greasing, as a gregarious driver bounced him along the town's rutted, dusty streets toward the Armijo Hotel. Along the way, the man pointed with his whip and suggested Longarm might want to try at least one night at the Columbian—a spanking-new all-brick affair recently erected on the corner of Main and Commercial.

"Lotta travelers are a makin' it known far and wide as how she's one of Colorado's finest new hostelrys," the genial fellow said. "'Course I ain't had nerve enough to even step a shit-covered boot in the place yet. But I'd bet a man of the world like yourself might find it exactly what the doctor ordered."

Fully aware of his financial limits as a government employee, Longarm declined the suggestion and waved the driver on to his original choice.

At the Armijo a snotty-looking, self-absorbed desk clerk, who sported a waxed moustache and oily hair, cast a wary glance at all the weapons the tall lawman carried and packed around his waist, then sniffed at the newly scrawled signature on the register. As daintily as an old maid at a tea party, he handed Longarm a key, then said, "Gettin' more'n our share of you heavily armed lawdogs pokin' around lately. Real famous one checked in yesterday. 'Pears as how he just might be in line for a deadly comeuppance while he's visiting with us."

"That a fact," the testy lawman spat back.

Taking no notice of the slight, the clerk continued. "Indeed, sir. We at the Armijo don't often entertain a man of Sheriff Pat Garrett's bloody fame."

"Pat Garrett's here?"

As though it were a well-kept, but widely known secret, the pretentious clerk surreptitiously pointed toward batwing doors in the wall opposite the registration desk. "Big as life and twice as deadly. Find 'im yonder in the bar. He's been a waitin' in there for almost an hour. Way I hear it, he's come to palaver with none other than Joe Antrim."

From somewhere in the back of Longarm's mind a spark of recognition flared. "Antrim? Faro dealer from Denver?"

The clerk leaned ever so slightly in Longarm's direction and whispered behind his ink-stained fingers, "Brother of the late Henry Antrim, a man also known as Billy the Kid—the notorious stock thief and killer from down Lincoln County way. The very one Sheriff Garrett killed."

For reasons he couldn't quite lay a finger on, Longarm had just never made the connection between the dull, humorless Denver gambler and New Mexico Territory's most famous rustler and murderer. He stared at the swinging doors. "Damn," he muttered, "ain't that a wonderment?"

The desk clerk enthusiastically nodded his agreement with the visiting lawman's assessment of the situation. "Appears as how you've arrived just in time for the big show, Marshal Long—whatever that might entail. Could be that Joe Antrim will kill Garrett graveyard dead, and we'll all get a rare opportunity to witness the entire gun-powder and blood-soaked dustup. Make a mighty fine tale to tell your grandkids, by God. Downright historical, don't you think?"

As he turned on his heel and headed toward the hotel's bar entrance, Longarm pitched a dollar gold piece onto the desk. It landed between the register's still open pages with a dull *thump*. "Have someone take my traps to the room. I'll be in the saloon."

The clerk snapped his newest guest's money up as though it might disappear in a puff of smoke and quickly deposited the coin into his own vest pocket. Sounding just a bit too unctuous, he said, "Why that exact duty is now my singular mission in this life, sir. I'll personally see to it my very own self, Marshal Long."

At the batwings, Longarm stopped, placed one hand on top of the swinging doors, and gazed into the murky, dimly lit depths. It took several seconds, but eventually his eye-sight adjusted to the darkened interior. He perused a narrow, oblong room with four tables on one side and a mahogany bar and mirrored back bar along the other. A long-legged, elegantly dressed, regal-looking gent sat in the farthest cor-ner near the street entrance. Nattily dressed in a three-piece suit, Pat Garrett appeared under no duress whatsoever, and leisurely sipped at a cup of steaming coffee.

A half dozen other customers stood randomly scattered around the primitive watering hole. Three had a spot in a tight knot at the end of the bar nearest Longarm's vantage point. Heads together, the trio whispered back and forth among themselves but appeared unarmed and thus, Long-arm determined, no real threat to Garrett or anyone else.

Longarm adjusted the heavy cartridge belt that sagged

under the weight of three pistols. All six of the saloon's miscellaneous drinkers amounted to nothing more than some of Trinidad's local gawkers, he thought. Then he boldly stepped into the saloon and strode in the direction of Garrett's table. About halfway across the room, he removed his hat and extended a friendly hand.

Lincoln County's famed former lawman broke into a smile. "Just be damned. Now here's a pleasant surprise. Mighty good to see you, my old compadre. Mighty good," he said, as he stood, while they shook hands. "When did you get into town, Custis?" The soft, rolled sounds of Chambers County, Alabama, permeated Garrett's voice and conjured visions of the antebellum South.

"Mighty good to see you, too, Pat. Came in from Denver on the D&RG 'bout an hour ago."

Garrett patted Longarm on the upper arm and gently urged him toward a chair. "Well, come on now, sit. Sit. Have a beer, glass of your special brand of rye, or maybe a cup of coffee. As you can see, I've got my own pot. We'll parley a spell."

Longarm eased into a ladder-backed, cane-bottomed chair designed specifically to torture a man's behind, then pitched his hat onto the badly worn, felt-topped table. As if by magic, an obviously nervous, chunky-gutted bartender carrying a towel over one arm instantly appeared at his elbow. The twitchy-eyed, drink wrangler ceremoniously rearranged everything on the table, then made quite a show of slapping away any invisible crumbs.

"What's your pleasure, mister?"

"Double shot of Maryland rye, if you've got it. If not, I'll take a beer, but only if it's nice and cold. Failing that, I'll have a cup of my friend's coffee."

The moon-faced liquor slinger flashed an uneasy grin. "Double shot of Maryland rye comin' right up, sir," he said and hustled back to the bar.

Longarm tapped the tabletop with one finger. "You've done gone and got some famous here of late, Pat."

Garrett shook his head, cast a distracted glance at the ceiling, then ran a hand from forehead to chin. "Swear 'fore Jesus, I never meant to be famous, Custis. Not the way it all eventually shook out anyhow. Was just tryin' my best to go along and get along, from one day to the next."

"Ain't that the way with all of us, Pat?"

Garrett leaned forward and crossed his arms on the tabletop, as though about to share the answer to one of life's more difficult mysteries. "You know, years ago I heard a feller say, 'If you ever have a life's choice between bein' rich or bein' famous, for the love of God, pick rich.'" He sagged back into the chair, toyed with his coffee cup a second, then added, "I can authoritatively say, I now know exactly what that windy-mouthed son of a bitch meant. Give a helluva lot, this very minute, to be rich instead of somethin' borderin' on legendary."

"Well, you mighta thought about the consequences of your actions before you went and killed the hell out of Billy Bonney or Henry McCarty or Henry Antrim or whatever in hell the vicious little buck-toothed bastard's actual fuckin' name was."

Garret grimaced, took a sip from his steaming cup of up-and-at-'em juice, then spat, "You hit that one right on the head, amigo. Damned eastern publishing establishment has put out an absolutely grotesque amount of silly-assed misinformation, and downright bullshit about that ugly, rat-faced dwarf. Includin' all the things he did, or didn't do, how he died, and me. I'd be more'n willing to bet you can't find a handful of people living in the entire country who know the true and actual story of Billy the damned Kid and why he ended up deader'n a rotten fence post, with my bullet in his chest."

Longarm glanced at the tabletop and noticed a full glass of rye near his elbow. He'd been so focused on Garret's rant that the bartender's stealthy delivery of his order had completely gone unnoticed. He took an abbreviated sip of the potent liquor and smacked his lips. "Well, Pat, as my dear ole white-haired pappy used to say, most people only know what they read, or what they make it a point to find out."

"You know, Custis, I've about come to the conclusion that *most people* today are fuckin' idiots. 'Bout ninety percent of the illiterate masses can't tell their assholes from their elbows. Vast majority of those who can tell the difference appear more than willing to believe any windbag who happens along to blow goat-feathers their direction, and manages to sound about half-assed intelligent. Worst of 'em is the fuckin' politicians. All stripes and kinds. Lyin' sons of bitches, every damned one of 'em."

Appearing deep in thought, Longarm twirled his drink around in the wet spot under the glass. "Well, you could write your own account of the entire Billy Bonney incident. Clear everything up on your own, as it were."

Garrett stared at Longarm as though pleased with the suggestion. A satisfied smile spread over his heavily moustachioed face. "Strange you should mention such an, endeavor, Custis. I've recently given a goodly amount of thought to doing exactly that. My old friend Ash Upson, who's a former ink slinger, and knew the Kid back in Silver City, claims to have knowledge of Bonney's origins and such. He's agreed to help me flesh out a factual rendition of all the events surrounding the Kid's demise—based on my personal recollections of course. I hope, by God, our combined efforts will, finally and forever, set the record straight. Maybe dispel some of the hero worshipping horse shit that's come out of that murdering little weasel's much-deserved death at my hand."

Longarm nodded, slipped a cheroot from his inside vest pocket, and fired it up. He flipped the smoking match toward a spittoon, then took another fiery sip from his glass. "Sounds like a damned fine idea to me, Pat. You get the book published, promise I'll buy a copy. Even read it if'n you'll sign it for me. Swear I will."

Garrett cast a tired glance around the room. "I could sure enough use the money a book might generate right now. Governor of New Mexico refused to pay me the five hundred dollar reward posted on the Kid's grubby, ambushing little ass. Territorial legislature's supposed to fix that particular oversight shortly. Sure as hell hope it comes to pass."

"Hear you've got more pressing problems than a possible book deal right at the moment," Longarm offered. "Strolled in here from the hotel's registration desk to find out if you might be in need of some help 'fore the day's out."

Garrett waved a dismissive hand. "Joe Antrim's in town's all. Claims he's Billy's brother—far less dangerous and perhaps a bit smarter. Not much of a gun hand from what I've been able to determine. But I'll be careful not to let him get behind me anyway. Supposed to meet with him later on today." He fished a gold watch the size of a hard-boiled egg from his vest pocket, glanced at it, then slipped the timepiece back into its hiding place. "Fact is he's a few minutes late as we speak. Guess maybe my brain's running

44

a bit slow today as well. He's nothing much to worry about, really."

Longarm glanced around the room to make sure all the players still occupied the same spots. "Sure you don't want me to stick around and watch your back?"

For the first time Garrett offered up a smile laced with warmth and depth. "It's damned nice of you to offer, Custis, but completely unnecessary. I don't foresee the least problem with Joe to tell the truth. Figure he just wants me to fill him in with the true facts of how his wayward brother bit the big one. Bein' as how he wasn't within five hundred miles of the event, he knows just about as much as any newspaper-writin' asshole does, and just can't wait to tell me all about it."

The balance of Longarm's Maryland rye slashed across the back of his throat and the empty glass hit the table with a thud. "In that case, I do have some pressing matters to discuss with Trinidad's city marshal."

A look of concerned interest crossed Garrett's face. "Mason Dobbs? What kind of business do you have with Dobbs? Man could easily lay claim to being one of the worst lawmen in the West. Well, if not the dead-level worst, surely the laziest."

Longarm's face split into a grin. "You always were one for the truth, Pat, even if it was like bein' slapped in the face with a wet bar rag. Dobbs claims to have seen, or maybe that someone might have spotted, the one and only Spook Lomax skulkin' around Trinidad."

"Spook Lomax. Do tell." Garrett shook his head. "Now there's one murderous skunk that'd drive a Baptist preacher to cussin' a blue streak. Man's a helluva lot worse than Billy Bonney ever thought about being. Never knew Bonney to kill folks by choppin' 'em into several pieces while they were still alive."

Longarm stood and offered his hand again. As the men shook he added, "My sentiments exactly, Pat."

"Be careful out there, Custis."

"Do my level best, amigo. Now, as long as you're comfortable with the situation today, think I'll mosey on down to the marshal's office. No need to keep Dobbs waitin' any longer. Maybe we'll meet up again 'fore you have to hit the trail."

Garrett nodded. "Maybe we will, Custis. Certainly hope so. Before you go, though, want to know something odd, amigo?"

"Go ahead, Pat. I've got a minute."

A deep sadness seeped into Garrett's voice when he shook his head, then said, "Back before I had to start chasin' Billy Bonney all over hell and New Mexico Territory, I actually liked the boy. But ever since I killed the little bastard, I've grown to hate him more every day for what he's managed to do to me since his passin'. Strange, ain't it?"

Longarm stared down at his friend and said, "I don't think so, Pat. Doubt anyone else would either." Then he turned and headed for the hotel lobby.

As Longarm stepped through the batwing doors, he came nigh running all over Joe Antrim, who single-mindedly pushed his way past and headed for Garrett's table. The Denver gambler's grim, beady, rodentlike eyes were completely glazed. He seemed like a man who'd just looked into the depths of a fortune-teller's crystal ball and foreseen his own departure from this earthly vale of tears.

Longarm turned and watched as an obviously nervous Antrim approached the man who'd killed his brother.

Garrett didn't rise, and made no offer to shake the gambler's hand. He motioned toward the empty chair Longarm had only recently vacated. Antrim slid into the seat like a chastised child who'd just been caught out behind the barn playing with himself. Garrett glanced toward the batwings, winked, and touched the brim of his hat.

Longarm nodded, then turned, heeled it for the street, and headed out in a search for Mason Dobbs's office.

Chapter 5

Trinidad's city marshal, Mason Dobbs, skittered across his office and away from Custis Long like a Louisiana crawdad running from a hungry Cajun. The hatchet-faced, thin-as-a-fence-picket badge-toter made an obvious point of putting a run-down desk between himself and the Denver-based federal lawman before he whined, "Musta been some kinda erroneous misinterpretation of that there wire I sent to Marshal Billy Vail. Never said I *seen* Spook Lomax my very own self, mind you. Just made mention of the fact that could be other folks hereabouts had reported as how they'd spotted a tall, skinny, pale-as-death, pink-eyed feller in the company of as many as six other men, a prowling around these parts."

Red-faced, with a growing antagonism, Longarm advanced on the desk and shook his finger in Dobbs's face. "Look, you spineless snake, I have neither the time nor the inclination to bandy words with brainless twits like you about what might or might not have been what you actually said to Marshal Vail in a telegram. Tell me right this instant where, precisely, did whoever it was who thinks he, or she, mighta spotted the phantom albino in question, imagine that he, or she, possibly saw the murderous slug?"

Dobbs took on the aspect of a puzzled puppy, mystified by Longarm's deeply and deliberately convoluted question. The bewildered town marshal's head tilted to one side, and he tapped his chin with a nervous finger. "Well, it mighta been a soiled dove of my acquaintance name of Three-Toed Alice McCoy. She works out'n a house over on the end of West Main—our Devil's Addition, you see—the Tenderloin-Trinidad's version of Hell's Half Acre. Thinkin' on it though, guess as how it coulda actually been her pimp—he's a feller I've had a few drinks with, but I only know him as Stick-Pin Johnny. Wears a big ole diamond on a gold pin stabbed through his cravat. Or, if it comes right down to the nub of it, coulda been . . ."

"Dammit, Dobbs," Longarm growled, "you'd better be gettin' to the name of the person I need to speak with and right damned soon. If you've got a heartless butcher roamin' the streets, we'd best do somethin' right quick 'fore citizens start dyin' right, left, and center."

Dobbs flinched as though he'd been slapped. "Talk to Johnny and the girl—Three-Toed Alice. They's the ones what come to me with the story 'bout the albino feller. Yep, that's the ticket."

Longarm glared at Dobbs and watched as the man fidgeted from foot to foot. He looked like he was in desperate need of a trip to the nearest outhouse. "Don't shit me here, Dobbs," Longarm growled. "You're sure?"

"Oh, I'm absolutely positive, Marshal Long. Johnny said they was this here albino feller and three or four of his friends. Them boys really upset Johnny and the girl. Do believe they was the scaredest two people I've seen in years. But I couldn't make no whole lot of sense out of the tale they was a trying to tell. Anyway, I'll take you down to their crib myself, if'n you'd like. Alice works from a room in the Raton Pass Hotel. Be glad to hunt 'em up fer you. How's that sound?"

Longarm stepped back and nodded. "'Bout as fine as frog hair split six ways. Let's do it."

"Right now?"

"Hell, yes, right now. What'd you expect, Dobbs? Think I'm gonna sit on my ass here in Trinidad for a week waitin' for you to get around to doin' what you just offered?"

As Longarm and Dobbs picked their way along Trinidad's busiest thoroughfare, a constant, perambulating parade of cowboys, freight handlers, teamsters, gamblers, drummers, businessmen, drunks, whores, horses, and livestock of every imaginable description blocked any effort at steady progress. Several times the two do-rights were forced to a complete halt and required to wait for the movement of people and animals before they could proceed.

"Gets worse every day," Dobbs complained after he stumbled from the boardwalk and landed in a foot-deep bog of muddy water laced with every form of animal waste imaginable. "Noise level from the street most of the time is damn near deafening. Goddamned racket goes on day and night. Seems like the whole of humanity and all their livestock is a movin' north right through Trinidad along this fuckin' street. Smells downright intolerable on days when the temperature gets any higher'n fifty degrees."

Longarm cast a glance at the churning morass of people and animals crowded around them. "No doubt about it, Dobbs, your town's busier'n a squad of bartenders on payday, for damned sure."

Dobbs stopped on the boardwalk long enough to toe at an unconscious drunk who had passed out in the doorway of a butcher shop. He got no response. "You know, Marshal Long, they's a good chance Stick-Pin Johnny and Three-Toed Alice have already packed up their meager belongings and headed out for the next boomtown of any consequence. People the likes of them two don't stay put very long in any one place."

"You get me to where you last saw 'em. I'll take care of everything from there," Longarm said, then pushed an obviously inebriated beggar out of his way.

The tramp, his grit-smeared, empty palm still extended, refused to give up on the possibility of money in hand and stumbled drunkenly along the teeming walkway a step and a half behind the two marshals. "All I want's jus' a got-damn dollar, mister. Hell, that ain' askin' too much. I'm hongery. Ain' had nothin' to eat in two fuckin' days. A dollar for the love of Chris'. Come on, now. You look like a feller who's got plenty. Leas' you could do is share a little of the wealth with them who'er less forsh-nate. Have pity on those as are in need, you son of a bitch."

Outside the door of the Raton Pass Hotel, a burly bouncer sporting a ratty felt hat and a three-piece suit that looked several sizes too small nodded his acquiescence. He easily granted the two lawmen entry, but then grabbed the tramp by the seat of his ragged, mud-encrusted pants and hustled him away.

Over his shoulder the drunk called out, "Jus' a got-damn dollar you stupid cocksucker. S'all I needed."

Longarm followed Dobbs to the registration desk, then stood to one side and listened while Trinidad's marshal spoke with the dilapidated inn's surly clerk. "How's it hangin', Mort? Don't mean to bother you none, but I'm needin' a bit of important information. Wonderin' if Stick-Pin Johnny and Alice are still around these days?"

The hotel's toothless, corpulent keeper of the ledger,

who appeared to have never met the tiniest morsel of food he didn't immediately shove down his gullet, was draped over the reception desk like a fleshy snowbank. Given the odor that oozed from the clerk's direction, Longarm decided the man had evidently never met a soap-and-water bath either.

The stinking, blubbery slug eyeballed Longarm as though he'd discovered a horse fritter the size of a Mexican sombrero in his coffee. After several unresponsive seconds had passed, he turned back to Dobbs and grumbled, "Yeah, they's still workin' the streets at night and sleepin' all god-damn day. Him and that crazy slut a his is up in Room 205, far as I know, or give a twelve-pound shit. Top of the stairs and to your left, gents. Try not to disturb our other *guests*. They need their rest."

Dobbs led the way up the rickety staircase. When they stopped at the door to Stick-Pin Johnny's room, Longarm cast a suspicious glance up and down the hallway, then said, "The Armijo's nigh on to a European palace compared to this dump. Place like this 'un makes me mighty glad I'm carryin' three pistols."

Unfazed, Dobbs lightly tapped on the door with two knuckles, then said, "Nothin' but transients, pimps, killers, and whores here, Marshal Long. Absolute dregs of the world. Manager of the Armijo wouldn't allow any of these folks to set a foot in his lobby 'thout havin' his bouncer kickin' the hell out of 'em."

From inside the room a man called out, "Get the fuck away from my door, you thick-headed bastard. Lest you want your incredibly ignorant ass kicked so hard you'll have to unbutton your fly to eat."

"See here, now, it's City Marshal Dobbs, Johnny. Need to talk with you and Alice 'bout that albino feller you seen."

A long silence from behind the door followed. The voice sounded nearer the still-closed and locked portal when the man shouted, "No time. No time today. We're extremely busy, Marshal. You'll have to come back tomorrow, or maybe the next day. Some other time. Hell, any other time but now."

Longarm stepped forward and whacked the door so hard with the butt of his strong-side pistol it rattled on its rusted hinges. "I'm a deputy U.S. marshal, you stupid son of a bitch, and I'm orderin' you to open this door. If it's not opened in five seconds, I swear 'fore Jesus, I'll kick it down, then I'll kick your stupid ass till your nose bleeds."

Almost immediately the bolt slid back and the lock snapped open. A narrow crack appeared as the plank door moved. A haggard, unshaved strip of a man's face and one eye appeared in the newly revealed crack. "Me'n Alice ain't got nothin' to say 'bout that albino feller, or any of them as was with him. Not a damned thing. You understand?"

Longarm pushed the door open, strode past the quaking Stick-Pin Johnny and into an ill-lit, airless, dreary room that smelled of sweat, crusted filth, burned tobacco, human waste, and that strange, sickly sweet odor of impending death.

A near-naked, red-haired woman, who looked to be fully able to crawl through a stovepipe without getting any soot on her, lay stretched across the shabby bed on her stomach. On first glance she appeared not to be alive, but all of a sudden the skin-and-bones female sucked in a huge, slobbery, ragged breath and attempted to raise herself from a mountain of grimy bedsheets and soiled clothing. As she flopped to one side, Longarm noticed that several toes were missing from one of her feet.

Stick-Pin Johnny, an equally skeletal, six-foot-tall,

weasel-faced bundle of tightly wrapped, raw nerve ends, danced from foot to foot. Then he went to mining for gold somewhere within the depths of the cod piece of his bal-briggans. A grit-covered finger, finding no hidden riches in his crotch, darted up to his nose, then proceeded to exca-vate around inside his skull. He took the time to carefully inspect what he'd found, wiped the shining, offensive par-ticle away on his underwear, then said, "Look here, fellers, like I tole you before, neither of us ain't got nothin' to say. Sides 'at 'er albino feller tole me, as how if'n we was asked, not to go blabbin' 'round 'bout him and his friends. Creepy cocksucker and them four yellow-toothed demons he had with 'im come near scarin' me'n poor Alice right slap to death. Hell, she ain't been the same since him and his boys was here. Have to admit, I'm beginnin' to get some worried 'bout the girl. Acts like she's gone sickly, or somethin'."

Longarm slipped the pistol back into its holster and set the hammer thong in place. "Well, Johnny, my friend, you've already violated a sadistic killer's personally deliv-ered instructions on how to keep your stupid self alive and healthy. Be willing to bet the farm that if Spook Lomax were to somehow discover what just came out of your dim-witted mouth, your sorry hide wouldn't be worth a plug of used chewing tobacco."

Three-Toed Alice's twitching pimp went white in the face. His bloodshot glance darted over to the girl on the bed. She blindly struggled to sit up, puked in her own lap, then rolled over in the gruesome mess. Johnny's eyes blinked so fast they appeared totally out of control. "Well . . . uh . . . I . . . uh . . . look you fellers wouldn't go an' tell 'im I said anything, now would ya? He's a crazy sumbitch, you know."

Longarm held up a reassuring hand. "We won't say a word. But we do need to know what they wanted and what they said and did while they were here."

Johnny darted to a chest of drawers standing against the wall at the end of the bed, snatched up a half-empty bottle, took a sloppy swig, then wiped liquor dribbles away with the back of his arm. Pained sadness and real regret laced his voice when he said, "Five of 'em wanted Alice all at the same time. They 'uz willing to pay right handsome for their pleasures, too. Made me an offer in gold I couldn't turn away, you see. Don't know exactly what they done to 'er. She wouldn't, or couldn't, say afterward. Tried to get it outta her, but she clammed up soon's them boys was done. Ain't said much a nothin' since. Begin' to get worried 'bout her, you know. She looks bad, doncha think? Acts bad, too."

Dobbs pointed at the unconscious girl. "Can she talk at all?"

Stick-Pin Johnny shook his head. "Ain't said nothin' in a coupla days. Been busted out on the laudanum and the whiskey ever since Lomax and his boys got done with 'er. Don't think she could tell you much of anything even if she could talk. My guess is all they did was take turns a-goin' at 'er. Worked her over for almost two hours. Like I said, they paid good, but near as I can tell the whole damned bunch of 'em more'n got their money's worth."

Longarm slapped the butt of the pistol strapped high on his right hip. "They're extremely bad men, Johnny. Spook Lomax is a wanted murderer, more'n a dozen times over, and has a cash price on his head. Most likely his *generous* friends do as well. I need to find all of them before they can hurt or kill anyone else. Did you hear 'em say anything that might be helpful?"

Stick-Pin Johnny looked puzzled for a moment, then shook the fingers of one hand as though they were on fire. "Not really, but last night I seen two of 'em as went at Alice a drinkin' at the bar over in the Matador Saloon. Wasn't the first time neither. Think all them boys spends considerable of their time drinkin' somethin' somewheres."

Dobbs sounded surprised when he jumped in before Longarm could speak and said, "You're sure about that, Johnny?"

"'Course I'm sure. One feller had an eye that's done gone missin'. Wore an ugly black patch over the hole the misplaced orb left behind." He ran a finger along his jaw from ear to chin. "Other'n has an awful-lookin' scar on his face. Thick, pink ribbon of lumpy flesh. Looks like somebody hacked on his face for a spell with a well-stropped straight razor. Both of 'em evil-eyed hard cases. You don't forget men like that once you've seen 'em. And I swear, Marshal, they 'uz over at the Matador last night. Almost all night long, as a matter of pure fact."

"Be damned," Longarm said, snorting. "Wonder if they'll be back tonight? Wouldn't doubt it."

Dobbs looked puzzled for a second, then said, "You know 'em, Marshal Long?"

Longarm scratched his chin, then, as though to himself, said, "Possibly. Just could be. In fact more than could be." He took one step toward the door, but stopped and turned back to the edgy pimp. "What were you doin' in the Matador last night, Johnny?"

"I 'uz tryin' to drum up some business for Alice."

Longarm's eyes narrowed. "You just said she hasn't been herself in days—barely speaks. Shit, don't have to be a sawbones to know the woman looks like she's knockin' on death's door. Why would you be out tryin' to drum up business for a whore who appears too far gone to even wiggle?"

Stick-Pin Johnny smiled like a gopher in soft dirt. "Hell, most fellers 'round here could care less if'n a willin' woman is even conscious or not. Good many of 'em wouldn't give two shits if she was livin' or dead. Fact is, Marshal, you could turn me loose on West Main for as little as ten minutes and it'd be no chore a'tall to find you fifty men who'd hump a stone-cold dead woman just as quick as a live one. Pussy's pussy far as most is concerned."

Three-Toed Alice rolled onto her back and went into a coughing, gagging, I'm-gonna-die-right-here-if-somebody-don't-help-me fit. Johnny darted to her side, brought the distressed woman to a sitting position, and did as much as he could to help. Most of his efforts involved slapping the poor woman on her hollow-sounding back. For about a second, Longarm marveled at the tenderness the scruffy pimp displayed toward his meal ticket. Then, he hit the door in a semi-trot and headed back down the stairs for the street.

Once on the bustling boardwalk again, an agitated Mason Dobbs hovered at Longarm's elbow. Shifty-eyed, he watched as the deputy U.S. marshal fired a cheroot and sucked down a long, deep, head-clearing lung of the smoke.

"Well, Marshal Long, what now?"

Longarm puffed on the cigar and squinted into a low-hanging, bloodred sun. "Where's the Matador Saloon, Dobbs?"

More than a bit of reluctance showed as Trinidad's piss-poor example of a lawman raised his bony arm and pointed five or six storefronts down and across West Main Street. "Yonder. Disreputable in the extreme, Marshal Long. Close to bein' the rowdiest joint in town. Matador's on a steady path of two or more bloody shootin's a week. Been

58

a number of vile killin's over there. Feller name of Brutus Claggett runs the place."

"Brutus Claggett, huh? Sounds like a real pleasant sort. Bet he goes to Sunday school every time the church house doors open. Wait, you know, think I might have made his acquaintance up in Silver City at some point. If he's the man I'm thinkin' of, he's tougher'n a wild hog's snout."

Dobbs wrung his hands and swayed from foot to foot like a tree in a stiff breeze. "He's a hard 'un for damned sure, Marshal Long—a real bucker and snorter. Ain't no secret as how he cultivates the company of a rowdy crowd. It's common knowledge that the Matador's got some of the most vicious sons of bitches you can imagine hangin' around over there. Most times me and my deputies don't even go near the joint, lest they's a killin' takes place, or some other equally awful act gets done that requires an appearance by representatives of the law."

Longarm slipped the Frontier model Colt from the cross-draw holster mounted high on his left hip. He flipped the loading gate open, rolled the cylinder, checked each shell, then carefully did the same with each of his other two pistols. As he replaced the weapon carried at his back, he snatched the cigar from the corner of his mouth, then turned to Dobbs and said, "No need for you to go with me, Dobbs. Might as well trundle on back to your jail. I'm pretty certain it's relatively safe there. Anything amiss takes place, you'll surely hear about it."

Dobbs pulled his flat-brimmed hat off and ran trembling fingers through thin, rust-colored hair. "While I do appreciate you thinkin' of my safety, wish you'd reconsider," he said, then slapped the hat back on his sweaty head. "Sure would hate to be the one what has to send Billy Vail a telegram about your untimely demise."

Longarm stepped off the boardwalk and headed back into the inexorable tide of animals and people moving west along West Main Street. He dismissively waved at Dobbs over his shoulder and called out, "Billy knows exactly why I'm here and how I go about my business, Dobbs. So don't worry 'bout me. Get on back to the jail and keep yourself safe."

Through beady, ratlike eyes, Trinidad's nervous marshal gazed down at Longarm from his slightly elevated position on the boardwalk. Several times he glanced up at the churning, ink-colored, lightning-laced clouds overhead and fidgeted, as though unable to make up his mind exactly what should be done. His face was creased with the solemn, pained aspect of a person certain he was staring at a dead man.

Finally, Dobbs shrugged like a beaten man, then ducked his head and scuttled away. Under his breath, he said, "Go on ahead and get your big dumb ass kilt for all I care. Tried to warn you. Ain't no man can say I didn't. Gonna get to my desk and write all this down quick as I can. Ain't no blame gonna fall on my head 'cause you're an idiot, Deputy U.S. Marshal Custis By God Long."

Chapter 6

Behind a set of well-used batwing doors painted a glorious rust-colored red that resembled dried blood, the Matador Saloon heaved and throbbed as an ocean of humanity swept in and out like storm-tossed pebbles on a rocky, windswept beach. Longarm pushed his way into the smoke-drenched cathedral dedicated to drunken people, public sex, noise, music, laughter, shouting, angry belligerence, and the distinct feeling of life on the very edge. A place where life was as cheap as ten-cent-a-shot rotgut whiskey and as easy to lose as bad bets at a crooked roulette wheel. It was the kind of joint where some attendees, at any particular evening's service, held life as cheaply at half the price of a used boot.

Longarm elbowed past knots of faithful worshippers gathered around a variety of gambling devices. Each whirl of the wheel or fall of the card was designed to take even the most careful man's money in record time. In the farthest corner from the door, opposite a three-man band—rinky-tink piano, twangy banjo, and a brassy, dented trumpet—he found a battered table occupied by a semiconscious drunk who had puked all over himself.

From all appearances, the intoxicated man hadn't breathed a sentient, sober breath in at least a month. Longarm grabbed the back of the near insensible inebriate's chair and dragged the barely breathing mound of bar squeezin's as far away as he could, then left the man sitting in the middle of the room like a misplaced chamber pot.

Pleased with his minimal efforts at housekeeping, Longarm strode back to the chosen corner, dropped into a chair, and waited. The way he had it figured, news that a deputy U.S. marshal was on the prowl would get around pretty quickly. Someone would surely come by to check on him—sooner or later. He hoped for Brutus Claggett, but was more than ready to settle for anyone inclined to make himself available for questions.

Within a minute after settling into the painfully uncomfortable chair, a burly, slick-headed bartender pushed through the seething crowd and eased up to Longarm's chosen pew. Sweat glistened on the man's shining, hairless dome. Ugly yellow pools of liquid drenched his filthy shirt and spread from under his arms like a pair of unchecked, watery growths. He snatched a damp towel from his beefy shoulder and slapped at the table as though trying to knock away invisible crumbs, dead bugs, or whatever else might have accumulated there.

"What'll it be, mister?" the drink slinger grunted.

Longarm stared directly into the man's impassive eyes. "Tall glass a beer, if it's cold."

"Now, there's somethin' I wouldn't mind havin' myself. Sad to say, but right at the present, we ain't yet got the means to cool our beer off here at the Matador. Should be set up for the cold stuff in the next few weeks, but not right now. Gonna have to take it warm like everbody else, if'n you still want it."

"In that case, I'll have a double shot of Maryland rye. Best you've got."

"Now, that I can do. Think we've got a bottle of fine Gold Label behind the bar somewheres. That suit you?"

"Top drawer. Bring 'er on."

The barman turned and started away, but stopped when Longarm called out, "Where's Claggett?"

The sweat-beaded, bullet-shaped head swiveled around like the muzzle of a recently loaded and primed Napoleon cannon. Muscles in the man's jaws clenched and unclenched. In spite of the background noise, Longarm could hear the man's teeth grind. Black, emotionless button eyes, like those of a kid's corn-shuck doll, studied Longarm a bit more carefully.

"Oh, he's around, somewheres," the man grunted. "Not exactly sure I can pin him down for you right at the moment. But, yeah, he's around."

Longarm decided there was nothing to be gained by leaving any doubt in the creature's walnut-sized brain as to his intentions. He slipped his badge out of an inside coat pocket and flashed it. "Tell Claggett there's a deputy U.S. marshal name of Custis Long here next time you see 'im. Say I'd like to talk with 'im, at his convenience, of course."

With no outward display of emotion or overt acknowledgment, the barman's flat, black button eyes blinked several times. "You bet, Marshal. Yeah, I'll surely do that for you. Soon's I see 'im again. Be right back with your drink." Bullet Head turned back toward the bar, merged into the crowd, as though sucked down by a quicksand whirlpool, then disappeared from view.

Longarm pulled up another empty chair, then propped his feet on it. He fired a fresh cheroot and puffed it till the end glowed with fiery life. The still smoking match had barely dropped into a nearby spittoon, when a tall, dark, muscular brute with scarred eyebrows, flattened ears, and a crooked nose strode up like he owned the place.

Without invitation the creature took the only empty seat. For all his rough, outward appearance, Longarm's new table mate was dressed in a three-piece wool suit, fancy silk cravat, and sparkling white shirt. His fingernails were clipped and clean, and he appeared to spend an inordinate amount of time smearing greasy pomade in a head of thick, carefully combed iron-gray hair.

"I'm Claggett. Elton Crabbe, one of my bartenders, said you wanted to talk. What can I do you for on this fine evenin', Marshal?"

Longarm's feet dropped to the floor with a *thump*. He leaned forward and stared into Claggett's broad, heavily scarred face. "The moustache and chin whiskers are new, ain't they? Grew your hair out quite a bit longer, as well. Even stopped tryin' to color it. And from all available evidence, you've seen a bit more in the way of alley fights and barroom dustups, since last we met."

The saloon owner recoiled as though he'd been slapped in the face. "Don't have the least fuckin' idea what the hell you're talkin' about, lawdog."

Longarm smiled. "Oh yes, you do. You know exactly what I'm talkin' about, Oliver."

"Oliver? What in the name of sweet Judas are you rantin' on about, mister? Don't know you, and don't know any Oliver either."

"Oliver Alonzo Flowers. Been some years since we've seen each other, Oliver. Last time was when I dropped you off at the gates of the federal lockup in Fort Worth. Charge was mail theft as I remember. Stole a mailbag off the Fort Worth to El Paso stage. Kinda makes a man like me wonder just exactly how you've managed to get yourself back out here amongst the good people of Trinidad."

"My name's Claggett, you muddle-brained son of a bitch. Don't know nobody named Alonzo Flowers, and I ain't gonna argue the point with you, so get on with whatever'n the fuck you want from me."

Longarm leaned away from the table, propped his feet up again, then laced his fingers together and twiddled his thumbs. "Suit yourself—Alonzo. I didn't come here lookin' for an argument with you anyway, so just relax. What I need is some very important information. Guidance, as it were, from a man of your deep knowledge and experience. You steer me in the right direction, and I'll disappear right out of your life like a puff of tobacco smoke in a Kansas whirlwind. You'll forget I was ever here quicker'n a bad dream."

Red in the face, Claggett puffed up like a stomped-on bullfrog, grumbled under his breath, then went to picking at a splintered spot in the tabletop. "Well, get on with it. Figured you got me over here for somethin'. What's your pleasure, *Marshal*?"

"Lookin' for Spook Lomax. You tell me how to find the murderin' piece of incredibly white trash, and I'll vanish so fast a week from now you won't even remember this conversation ever took place."

Claggett squirmed in his chair, which squeaked and complained like the seat under his ample ass had suddenly heated up. "Spook Lomax? Hell, I don't know where Spook Lomax is. In point of actual fact, I don't know anyone named Spook Lomax. And even if I did, not sure I'd bother tellin' the likes of you. Like everyone else, I've heard wild stories as to how the man ain't averse to killin' the hell outta anyone what crosses him, but I don't know him."

"Last night men who fit the descriptions of Henry Hatchett and Frank McCabe spent nigh on the entire evening drinking at your bar. Bother to notice either one of them? They're some pretty bad types. Have reputations for evil doin's all over this part of the west. And they're runnin' buddies of ole Spook. Fact is, he might be traveling with as many as six others just as bad as Hatchett and McCabe."

"So? You gonna make a federal case out of men drinking at my bar? Hell, I wouldn't know either one of 'em if'n the cocksucker walked up and took a piss on my feet. A saloon owner can't know everyone who frequents his place of business."

"Understand that, but these are men who carry a reputation themselves. I know they were here, and figure you're fully aware of their visit."

"Look around, Marshal. This joint's packed. Men come and go in droves. Cowboys, gamblers, miners, drummers, herders, hell, you put a name to 'em and they're here at one time or another. They come for the liquor, the gamblin', the whores, the companionship, a quick blow job, or something to eat from our free sandwich platter on the bar. Hell, I make my livin' providin' whatever a man can think of to yearn for. Get you a blow job for free if'n you'd like."

Longarm leaned closer and locked the arrogant saloon owner in a sharp-eyed gaze. "It can wait. Hatchett and Mc-Cabe are both wanted men. Didn't exactly come to Trinidad for either of 'em, but I'll sure enough take 'em."

Claggett wasn't ready to be cowed. He shot a snarling glare back at Longarm and growled, "Done said it once, and I'll say it again, goddammit. Don't know either one of the sons of bitches. But it just don't matter anyway, 'cause

66

I don't give a royal shit if they murdered every Bible-thumpin' soul in Pueblo last night while all the hoople heads was on bended knees a prayin' in their churches. Long as them boys came in here and behaved while gamblin', buyin' liquor, samplin' some mighty fine pussy, or whatever in my saloon, I would not have had any reason to take note of their presence."

Longarm almost came out of his chair. From a threatening crouch, he shook a finger in Claggett's face and snapped, "That's just fine with me. Never did want to get in a man's way of doin' business. But don't you get in the way of me doin' mine while I'm here. Understood, you thickheaded bastard?"

The chair went over on its back with a muffled *thud* when Claggett shot to unsteady feet, made the snorting sound of a bull bison, then turned on his heel and stomped away. Just as the baldheaded bartender had before him, the Matador's outraged owner disappeared into the crowd like a drop of water sucked up by thirsty, sunbaked Mexican topsoil.

An hour passed, then two, then almost three. Longarm nursed a fourth glass of rye and continued to watch the crowd as it swelled, thinned, then swelled again.

About the time he'd made up his mind to give up the search and head back to the hotel for a much needed night's rest, he spotted One-Eyed Henry Hatchett and Scar-Faced Frank McCabe. The angry-looking outlaws bulled through the Matador's batwing doors, then hesitated long enough to scan the churning throng.

In barely a ticked second, the scruffy pair's combined gazes fell on Longarm like burlap bags filled with boat anchors. Hands hidden from view by the tabletop, Longarm slipped both hip pistols out of their well-oiled holsters unnoticed. He cocked the weapons and slumped backward into his chair, as though nearly drunk or simply relaxed and almost asleep. He let the guns rest in his lap, and waited.

Even in a roomful of Trinidad hard cases, Hatchett's and McCabe's reputations preceded them, as though the bloody corpses of those they'd murdered marched in front of them. Both men commanded considerable immediate attention, and a well-earned degree of fearful respect.

"Be damned if Claggett didn't know they were here before," Longarm said to himself. "Lyin' bastard."

As if everyone in the seething saloon had suspicions of what was about to transpire, the multitude parted like the Red Sea for Moses.

Most of the drunken spectators appeared desperate to see whatever might eventually take place. They shuffled and pushed their way as far out of the perceived line of fire as possible and made every effort to pick a spot of relative safety where the view was still unimpeded. A very few— the smarter, almost sober ones—headed for the door and didn't let the batwings hit them in the ass as they hurriedly departed.

Longarm's eyes cut from one side of the room to the other. Near as he could tell, the saloon's more inquisitive customers appeared to feel there just wasn't anything that had the power to provide a bit of unexpected entertainment like the prospect of a brutal killing, or maybe even two or three.

For some reason a single voice cut through all the background clutter, and Longarm heard, "Jes' nothin' like blood and thunder. Hope these boys murder the shit outta this here lawdog. Ain't got a speck of love in my heart for any of 'em badge-carryin' bastards. Kill 'em all's what I sez, by God."

The sullen-faced pair of gunmen slowly jingled over to a spot less than ten feet from Longarm's table. An arm's-length apart, they rocked to a stop on their heels. Both men pulled heavy canvas coats away from holstered weapons, tilted backward for easy access. Everyone in the saloon possessed of any brains at all recognized the arrogant attitude oozing off the gunmen.

The belligerent pistoleers hooked their thumbs behind cartridge-studded gun belts and glared down at the object of their concentrated, three-eyed attention. All of a sudden, Trinidad's Matador saloon got quieter than the inside of an oyster on the bottom of the Atlantic Ocean. A whipcrack of tension snapped through the smoky air, and the smell of a bloody outcome seeped off Lomax's henchmen like dripping sweat.

Chapter 7

Longarm gauged the distance to the pair of gunnies and, beneath the table, leveled a pistol muzzle at the middle of each man. The inch-thick, felt-covered, wooden top might throw the shot off a bit, he thought, but it didn't really matter. The dumb sons of bitches had moved in so close he knew it shouldn't amount to much of a problem if, and when, the blasting started—whatever deadly dance they had in mind.

Red-faced and thick-necked, Henry Hatchett spoke first. "We done went and heard rumors as how you wuz a lookin' fer us boys, Mister Deputy U.S. By God Badge Toter. Just thought we'd stop on by and inquire as to what'n the blue-eyed hell you might want."

McCabe sounded like a gutsy echo when he grunted, "Yeah. Heard as how you're a lookin' fer us, you badge-totin' bastard. Wonderin'. Yeah, we wuz wonderin' some." Then the scar-faced maggot let out an odd, near insane-sounding little girl's giggle.

From beneath the brim of his Stetson, Longarm's gaze sliced back and forth through the dense curtain of tobacco smoke from one man to the other. Cold as a Montana well rope, he said, "Tell you, boys, best thing all around would be if you just dropped those pistol belts on the floor, then

71

heeled it on down to the jail with me. Sure to save you considerable discomfort."

Damned near toe-to-toe confrontation wasn't Longarm's usual cup of bitter tea, but he knew these two polecats weren't about to be placated or appeased. They were primed for a fight and didn't appear ready to back away. Hardheaded, arrogant belligerence was written all over each of their overconfident, hate-filled faces.

"Fat fuckin' chance," Hatchett snorted. "Ain't givin' up my gun for no-fuckin'-body. For damned sure ain't givin' my gun over to no lawman what's already let out word as how he's *lookin'* for me."

"Yeah, fat fuckin' chance," came the weird, giggling echo.

Longarm shook his head. "Well, boys, my immediate superiors didn't send me to Trinidad for either of you stupid sons of bitches. But as long as you've seen fit to seek me out and are standin' right in front of me, guess you'll have to do for the time being."

"You totin' paper on us, Marshal? You got wants, warrants, and such?" Hatchett growled.

"Nope, can't say as I do, Henry. But while the truth is I don't carry any open warrants on either one of you, I would be willing to throw down a goodly sum that you're both wanted for something somewhere. Likes of you fellers always are. And on top of everything else, it's my sworn duty to rid the countryside of murderous, theivin' scum of your widely reputed ilk."

McCabe's eyes came nigh to crossing. A look of total confusion swept over his face. "What the fuck's an ilk? Is that bad? He insult us, Hatch?" he mumbled.

Hatchett tilted his one-eyed head a bit farther back to his good side in search of a better view through the churning, hazy cloud that ebbed and flowed between and around the snarling antagonists. "An old friend of yern sent us over, lawdog. Sure you 'member Spook Lomax."

Longarm nodded. "We've met. Once. Very briefly."

"Spook done tole us as how you're somethin' of a feisty fucker, Long. A hard man to kill, Spook says. Said it sure would be good to hear that you was deader'n a rotten willow stump. Tole him as how it didn't matter one whit how feisty you was to me. See, I done kilt more'n my share of them as would be nervy enough to think they was feisty. From all available appearances, looks to me like killin' you oughta be 'bout as easy as usin' a rockin' chair."

McCabe's crazed, snorting giggle got even weirder and more pronounced. Like a man in the throes of the ague, he twitched and shook all over. "Doan look all that feisty to me neither, Hatch. I'd say this here marshal feller looks altogether like a dead man a sittin' at 'at 'ere table. And even if'n he ain't exactly dead right this very minute, think we can arrange for him to git undertaker-aged pretty quick like."

Hatchett plucked a thick, spike-shaped splinter of chewed wood from between rotted teeth. "Tell you, Frank, ain't never kilt me no deputy U.S. marshal afore. But, you know, they's a first time for damned near everthang. Leastways that's what my dear, sainted, ole white-haired granny always used to tell me."

McCabe cut a sqinty-eyed, demented glance toward his partner, nodded like the bones in his neck had gone limp, then went for the pistol that hovered almost directly over his crotch. The poor-thinking gunman misgauged the time it would take to limber up the Cavalry model Colt from a holster that was clearly made for a shorter-barreled weapon. He panicked when the pistol's tall, unaltered front sight caught on the holster's open toe and wouldn't come loose.

"Shit," McCabe yelped, then threw a horrified glance back into his potential victim's slitted eyes.

Longarm squeezed off a thunderous shot that blasted a massive exit hole in the tabletop, and was immediately followed by a shower of flying splinters. The enormous piece of lead nicked one of the tiny bones as it passed through McCabe's right wrist, bored into the flesh of his side just above his cartridge belt, then punched a hole the size of a man's finger in his guts.

Deflected from its original course, the bullet plowed a deadly channel. It tumbled along a front-to-back path through the rest of the screeching man's body, then severed his spine. Covered in gore, it exited his back in a fist-sized spray of shattered bone, blood, and shredded material from the waistband of his pants.

Slowed by all its destructive travels, the now blunt-nosed slug dropped to the floor before it could reach the Matador's front door—located directly behind the spot where McCabe went to ground like a hundred-pound sack of fertilizer. The 255-grain ball left a bloody trail as it rolled to a stop against an overflowing spittoon that sat near the end of the bar against the brass foot rail. No one in the bug-eyed, gape-mouthed crowd who witnessed the shooting heard the metallic *plink* it made.

McCabe was a dead man before his limp body hit the floor. His still twitching corpse convulsively rolled onto one side, then he shit himself. Unseeing eyes popped open in permanent shock, then he puked up everything he'd had to eat in the prior two days.

Unnerved onlookers, by the score, set to yelling at the top of their lungs. A number of the stunned gawkers came nigh trampling each other to death when they hit the batwing doors in a seething, panicked knot. The drunken

74

crew screamed their way into Trinidad's busiest thorough-fare, where several fell and were almost stomped to death by the steady horse traffic passing in the street.

Some, lucky enough to occupy a handy spot near a lesser opening, headed for an almost invisible exit in a cor-ner of the back wall. A few raced one another up a cramped staircase to the second-floor landing. In an unthinking frenzy, they searched for the safety of a location away from the death-dealing gunfire and the possibility of their own eminent demise.

One man snatched up a chair and pitched it through the Matador's hand-painted front window, then jumped out the new opening, as shards of glass came down on his head like frozen rain. A number of the other horrified bystanders quickly followed the bold window jumper. Less than a minute after McCabe fell, only the boldest members of the original crowd of spectators remained.

A thick haze of spent, acrid-tasting, black-powder smoke rolled from under Longarm's splintered table. Stunned, Henry Hatchett threw up his hands and tried to scratch the Matador's elaborate, painted tin ceiling. "Oh, my Lord," he squealed. "Please don't shoot no more, Mar-shal Long. God Almighty, you done went and kilt poor, sad, dumb-assed Frank. Easy to see, for damned certain sure, you've already got me under the gun. Knew it soon's you blasted Frank. No need to kill me, too. Swear 'fore Je-sus, ain't no need to kill a pitiful one-eyed feller like me. I've been properly chastised already. Swear it."

The thunderous concussion from the pistol's muzzle blast had blown out a number of lamps hanging nearest Longarm's nest and set his ears to ringing like cathedral bells. The smoke and poor light made it somewhat prob-lematic to see clearly, but the huge vent created by the demolished front window was well on the way to remedying that situation.

Longarm brought both pistol-filled hands from under the table. The weapons were still cocked and ready for more in the way of deadly action. He rolled the muzzles at the only remaining assassin still standing. "Unbuckle that gun belt and let it drop, you son of a bitch," he snarled, then slowly pushed the chair back and got to his feet.

Ever cautious—he'd learned long before that even a dead rattler still had the hidden power to kill any man lacking the proper care—Longarm covered the twitching body of Scar-Faced Frank McCabe with the revolver in his left hand, Hatchett with the one in his right.

After considerable fumbling, and a good deal of loud swearing, Hatchett's bullet-studded pistol belt thudded to the sawdust-covered, rough-cut plank floor in a heap. Longarm flipped the barrel of his pistol in Hatchett's direction again, and said, "Now take your coat off, and be damned quick about it."

"Why?"

"Take your coat off, Henry, or I swear 'fore Jesus, I'll put one of these hot, blue .45-caliber whistlers in your right leg just above the knee. Old as you are, you'll never walk right again. Be a hobbling old man on a cane for the rest of your sorry life. That is, if you don't bleed to death from the wound."

Hatchett gritted his teeth, then set to stripping his knee-length coat away. "I'm a doin' 'er. I'm a takin' it off right now. Don't shoot, goddammit. Keep your head, Marshal. Don't want you to get any more agitated than you already are."

Eyeballing his every move, Longarm made Hatchett turn around in a complete circle before he finally holstered one pistol, then strode up behind the gunman and patted him down with the freed hand. "What's this, Henry?" he said, after he slapped the side of Hatchett's boot.

"Oh, nothin' really. Ain't much a'tall. Just a little ole two-shot derringer. Took it off'n a mean-assed whore down in Saltillo. Damned gal tried to put one in my skull with it. Use the little ole shooter for killin' rabbits, snakes, and such. You know, just in case I misplace my Colt."

Longarm stood. He pressed the open muzzle of his pistol against the back of Hatchett's head. "Slow as molasses in January, Henry, stoop down and fish that tiny popper out with your fingertips. Drop it on the floor, then stand up again—like you've got an anvil tied around your worthless neck."

Hatchett had barely gotten erect again when Marshal Dobbs slid into the Matador like a frog in a tack factory. Pistol in shaking hand, he stood with his back against the wall and called out, "Heard the shot. Figured you might need some help, Marshal Long. Got here quick as I could. Anything I can do for you in the way of assistance?"

Longarm grabbed Hatchett by the scruff of the neck and shoved him in the direction of Trinidad's skittish lawman. Hatchett stumbled, went to one knee, then wobbled back to his feet. "Take that son of a bitch down to your jail and lock his murderous, ambushin' ass up. I'll be along as soon as I can. Have more than a few questions I want to ask him later."

As a twitchy Mason Dobbs escorted his charge into the street and away from the scene, Longarm holstered his pistol, then bent over the bloody remains of Frank McCabe. A group of drink-carrying gawkers assembled in a loose semicircle around the corpse. They whispered and pointed as he rolled the body onto one side and gazed at the ragged hole where his well-placed shot had exited McCabe's back.

When the lifeless body accidentally slipped from Long-arm's grasp, it rolled flat onto its blood-soaked back. The still warm corpse made a curious gurgling sound that oozed up through the growing pool of black, sticky blood, gore, and minced tissue underneath in a frothy surge of pale bubbles. McCabe's open eyes blankly stared into space. The dead man's infamous scar, which ran along a sharp, angular jaw, Longarm noted, contained the only color left in the flesh of the man's entire, pale death mask of a face.

Longarm stood and glared down at the dead man. "Didn't want to kill you like this, Frank. Came after the man who sent you to do his dirty work. This whole ugly dance could've been avoided. Should've given up your gun and walked down to the jail with me. Least you'd still be alive, you stupid bastard."

One of the gandering drunks stepped up beside Long-arm and handed him McCabe's hat. "Found it over yonder under 'at 'ere table. Musta hit the floor and rolled quite a piece 'fore it came to rest against one leg. Thought you might want it." When the lawman didn't respond, the gawker drunkenly stumbled back to his knot of murmuring friends.

For some seconds Longarm stood over the leaking body and stared at the ceiling, as though looking heavenward for answers that didn't come. Finally, he held McCabe's hat out and dropped it over a graying face, tinted with the colors of violent death. "Yep," he said, "no doubt about it, Frank. You should've gone down to the jail with me. 'Cause you are, for certain, one dead son of a bitch now."

As he turned for the door, an ashen Brutus Claggett stepped from behind the bar and eased his way through the cluster of tipplers who'd seen the gunplay transpire. "Well, damnation. You sure 'nuff killed the hell out him, didn't you, Long?"

In a rush of movement that even surprised a man of Claggett's brutal background and sent him in a backward stumble until he was lodged against the bar, Longarm stormed up to the man till they stood almost nose to nose.

"Never cared much for killin' anybody, Claggett," Longarm growled right in the surprised saloon owner's face. "Even a skunk like ole Scar-Faced Frank over there. Have virtually no doubt you're the one who sent word to Spook that I was here. In reality, then, as far as I'm concerned, you're the one responsible for this mess. Seems to me you should clean it up. So, I'll leave you to it. Be damned sure he gets a decent burial, 'cause I'll be checking around to make certain you did as told."

Claggett got all bug-eyed and slobbery. "Damned if I will. Ain't about to pay for plantin' the son of a bitch, and you cain't make me, by God."

The barrel of Longarm's Frontier model Colt flashed out of its cross-draw holster. The heavy, seven-and-a-half-inch piece of blued steel bounced off the right side of Claggett's face in a single, bone-crunching swipe. Several of the surprised man's bloody teeth flew out of his mouth, hit the top of the bar, then ricocheted off a whiskey bottle. The Matador's owner dropped to the floor like a sack of dried seed corn thrown from the back of an Arkansas pumpkin roller's spring wagon.

With something akin to evil intent painted on his broad face, bartender Elton Crabbe rushed over, but found his nose inside the muzzle of Longarm's drawn pistol. "You tell this son of a bitch when he wakes up that I meant what I said. He'd best see to the buryin' of Frank McCabe at his earliest possible convenience. Otherwise, I'll come back over here and kick his ass till he'll have to unbutton his pants to sneeze."

Hands in the air, Crabbe muttered, "Yessir. I'll sure 'nuff do that, Marshal. See to it my very own self."

Longarm backed out of the Matador and into the street, where the night still contained a touch of what vaguely resembled fresh air, laced with the pungent aroma of horse shit. Once he'd managed to get safely across Trinidad's Main Street, he holstered his weapon, then stopped long enough to light a cheroot.

He shook his match to death, then glanced up at a bright, saucer-sized moon in a crystalline sky. The glittering orb was highlighted with a smattering of thin, stringy clouds. For a second, the surprised lawdog would have sworn that the skeletal face of death stared back at him from the icy, pale, lunar orb. A wave of chicken flesh crawled up his back and down his arms.

"Jesus," he mumbled to himself, "shoulda known all the lunatics would be runnin' loose on a night like this. Oh, well, now to see what One-Eyed Henry Hatchett has to say about it all."

Chapter 8

Longarm hit the jailhouse door like a Kansas cyclone and thundered his way inside. Mason Dobbs scampered for the perceived safety afforded by the sheltered spot behind his desk for the second time. Trinidad's pasty-faced lawman did a nervous foot-to-foot dance as the red-faced, deputy U.S. marshal flew across the office and jerked the steel-barred door to the cellblock open.

"Got 'im locked up, Marshal Long," Dobbs called out. "Done just like you tole me I should. But he ain't talkin' none. Ain't sayin' nothin', 'cept all 'bout how he ain't a gonna spill his guts to no federal badge toter. Claims as how we can use red-hot horseshoe tongs on the bottoms of his feet, rip out his toenails, or cut off his nose, and he says he won't give up nothin'."

Longarm stopped with one foot over the threshold of the cellblock doorway. "Did the son of a bitch bother to mention anything specific that he wouldn't talk about?"

"Well, as a matter of pure fact, did hear him say as how he 'specially ain't gonna say nothin' 'bout Spook Lomax. Then he bulled up, folded his arms, and informed me that there ain't no man livin' as can make 'im."

Longarm slumped against the cellblock's door frame, then scratched his chin. "Well, we'll just by God see about that," he said, then pointed to a set of shackles attached to a six-foot length of chain. The steel bindings dangled from a peg on the side of a well-stocked gun rack. "Put a chair in the middle of the floor. Get those cuffs ready. I'll bring Hatchett out of his cell. Once I've got him in here, gonna try and throw a scare into 'im. Maybe we can, at the very least, get enough in the way of information for me to track Lomax down 'fore he does any more real damage." He grabbed a ring of keys hanging from a square-headed nail in the wall beside the lockup entrance, then disappeared inside.

While Dobbs did as instructed, he heard One-Eyed Henry's cell door crash open, then Hatchett making pained, yelping sounds. Dobbs turned just in time to watch as the prisoner stumbled into the jail's outer office and crashed to his hands and knees like a kicked dog.

Hatchett crawled to the recently moved chair and pulled himself into it. He ceremoniously rubbed his knees, brushed some loose dust away from well-worn pant's legs, then barked, "Damnation, you law-bringin' son of a bitch. Sure as hell didn't have to go and knock me down like that."

Longarm leaned against the doorjamb. "Chain 'im to the chair, Marshal Dobbs. Make sure the bastard can't move around. 'Cause this dance is about to get bad ugly."

Hatchett's head snapped around and, with his one good eye, he glared at Dobbs, as though daring the skinny marshal to act on instructions he appeared to believe were incomprehensible. He shifted his fierce, ogle-eyed stare back to Longarm. "What in the blue-eyed hell are you up to, Long?"

With the prisoner's attention diverted, Dobbs hopped over to the chair like a scared rabbit and quickly snapped one cuff onto Hatchett's nearest arm. He looped the chain around the outlaw's ankles and the chair legs, then fastened the empty bracelet to Hatchett's remaining free wrist.

"What the fuck? Now this ain't right," Hatchett complained, then jerked against the uncomfortable steel bindings. "Ain't no need for such treatment, boys. Hell, you've got me. I'm your prisoner for certain sure. Already had me locked up. Pretty tight cage back there. I sure as hell wasn't a plannin' on goin' nowheres."

Longarm bent down, slipped a bone-handled, five-inch, Damascus-steel cowboy's knife from his boot top, then wiped the blade on the sleeve of his jacket. "Here's the way this hoedown is gonna go, Henry. I'll ask you some questions. If you don't give me the right answers, I'm gonna take your good eye." He made a brutal scooping motion with the knife's fancy, swirl-patterned blade. "Scrape the big brown sucker right out of the socket."

"You wouldn't, by God, dare," Hatchett grumped.

"Wanna bet your eye on that? Might even hand you one of those tin cups yonder by the coffeepot, and put your sorry ass out in the street to beg just like all them blind fellers in the King James Bible. Be interesting to see if you can collect any money, bein' as how you're already uglier'n a two-hundred-pound stack of hammered cow shit."

Hatchett's lips twitched, then curled back in an animalistic snarl from a mouth filled with rotten, crooked, yellow-stained teeth. His only eye swiveled around in its socket like an inquisitive owl's, then blinked several times. He shook a shaggy, lice-ridden head, then said, "Now, now, see here, that's total bullshit, Long. Ain't no sucha thing ever gonna happen. Man of your tender sensibilities wouldn't do a terrible thang like 'at. Would you?"

Longarm pushed himself away from the doorjamb. He

strode to within a step or two of the chained brigand; then stopped and used the knife to clean dirt from under one fingernail. "Oh, wouldn't I?" He leaned down so his face was on the same level with Hatchett's. "If I was you, Henry, I wouldn't make any serious wagers on that particular erroneous belief."

Hatchett tried to stand, but could only manage a tortured stoop. Longarm shoved him down again. In a motion that was so quick the prisoner flinched in disbelief, Longarm placed the knife point against Hatchett's cheek, then said, "Why were you, Frank McCabe, Spook Lomax, and at least four or five other evil sons of bitches, prowlin' around in Trinidad, Henry? What kind of wickedness were you boys up to before I got to town? Whatever you do, don't lie to me."

"Looka here, you know got-damn well that Spook'll kill me deader'n Davy Crockett, if I talk to you, Long. Swear 'fore Jesus, that man can dream up some of the worst ways to treat a human body you can imagine in your most harrowin' nightmares. If I tell you what you want to know, only God'll be able to figure out how this vale of tears will end for me. Most likely in several pieces. Man does love choppin' a body up."

Ever so lightly, Longarm twisted the knife tip against Hatchett's cheek. "Better get to tellin' me what I want to know and stop makin' excuses, Henry. Sure you've noticed by now, Spook ain't here. But by God, I am. And I'm the one holdin' the knife next to your only eye."

Beads of salty sweat formed on Hatchett's dirty forehead, ran into one scarred brow, then dripped onto a twitching cheek. "Well, now, look here, Marshal. How're you gonna know if'n I'm a tellin' you the truth, or not?"

Longarm pushed on the knife just enough to raise a drop

of blood and cause Hatchett to grimace. "I'll know, Henry. Trust me I'll know if you're lyin'. And if you're determined to be a blind man, just go on ahead and throw a bunch of windy whizzers, tall tales, and corral dust my way and see what happens."

Hatchett squirmed in the chair. He jerked at the chains again and moaned like a staked animal. It appeared to Longarm that the man had begun to leak sweat from every pore of his foul-smelling body. "He'll kill me, Long. You know I'm tellin' you true. Ole Spook'll cut me up like a butchered pig," he grunted. "I seen him chop a feller's head off one time with a double-bit ax. Stuck it on a heat-hardened pole, so's anyone passin' could see."

"You'll get no sympathy here, Hatchett."

"Have mercy, man. He's hung a number of ole boys for a helluva lot less than you're askin' me to do right now. Damn, he's even set livin' folks afire just to watch 'em burn. Wuz there when he set a pair of Pine Bluff watermelon farmers ablaze up in Arkansas a couple years back. Helluva nasty business. Made me sick to my stomach for days. Worst of it was the smell all them poppin' watermelons made as them poor burnin' boys cooked right in the field."

"All the whining in the world ain't gonna help you none, Henry. Might as well give me what I want."

Hatchett jerked at the chains. He tried to kick loose. Rocked the chair back and forth, then, all of a sudden, went limp all over. His head dropped and he moaned again. "Merciful God, don't do this to me, Long."

"Sorry, but I can't get you loose from your responsibilities this time, Hatchett. You've run your string out to its absolute end. Gonna have to give Lomax up, or go blind. Take your pick, but don't waste any more of my time."

The outlaw wagged his head from side to side like an old hound all crippled up with age and creeping arthritis. "Women." The word came out as a breathy whisper, then he added, "We come to town for some fresh women, damn your sorry, law-pushin' hide. On a good many occasions 'tween jobs, Spook would send some of us out a huntin' for women."

For the first time since Longarm's arrival in town, Mason Dobbs snapped to attention. He advanced to a spot within a foot or so behind the chained man. "What the hell was that you just said, Frank?"

Startled by the unexpected answer as well, Longarm took a step backward and pulled the blade off Hatchett's cheek and away from his eye. "Did I hear you right? You said women, didn't you, Henry? You came here for women?"

All of a sudden, Hatchett appeared tired all the way to the insides of his bones. His chin dropped to a heaving chest, as though he'd aged fifty years in a matter of seconds. "You heard me right. We come to Trinidad for new women, or at least one new woman anyways," he mumbled. "Spook gets bored with 'em pretty quick like, as you've already seen personal, Marshal." Hatchett glared up at Custis Long and let a knowing sneer curl his upper lip. "You know, he brags 'bout that 'un he kilt up on the Salt River. Loves to tell how he came nigh on blowin' your law-pushin' ass away."

Longarm's head snapped back like he'd been slapped. "Brags about it? He brags about what he did to Lydia Jefferys and her son up on the Salt?"

"Git 'im drunk and ole Spook dearly loves goin' over ever bloody detail of more killin's than most people could imagine in their most dreadful nightmares. Particular when

86

it comes to that'un on the Salt. Loves to wax eloquent 'bout the ax and how he sharpened it, then chopped them poor folks up. First the boy, then the woman. You know, he made her watch what he done to the kid."

"That's enough," Longarm growled. "I found 'em and don't need to be reminded about the butchery. Can't believe how wrong I've been ever since Billy Vail put me on this assignment. Figured for certain you boys were just out to pull another robbery, but stealin' women never entered my mind. Get on with it. Tell us the rest of why you're here now."

"Well, like I said, Spook decided as how he needed somethin' different. Pumps 'em once, maybe twice, and that's it. Acts like his dick's made outta gold or somethin'. The man's always lookin' for a fresh one, you know."

Through a pained expression, Dobbs said, "Fresh one? What the hell's that mean?"

For a second, Hatchett gazed at the ceiling as though praying, and almost as an afterthought he added, "Spook's got damned near an insatiable appetite when it comes to females, gents. God Almighty, I swear, he cain't seem to get enough of 'em. Always has us boys on the lookout for somethin' different. Creepy son of a bitch has a peculiar yen for them blond ones. Real or fake, don't matter to him. Sends us out searchin' for 'em blue-eyed, narrow-waisted, cute little gals. And Great God Almighty, I've seen the crazy son of a bitch just go bug-nutty over a redhead."

An absolutely horrifying thought popped into Longarm's chaotic brain. "How many of these female hunts have you been out on, Henry?"

"Don't remember for certain sure, Marshal. Three, four maybe." All of a sudden Hatchett's speech slowed. "Coulda been more." He shot a sneaky glance into Longarm's narrowed eyes, then tried to turn far enough to look over his shoulder at Dobbs. "Could be I shoulda kept my mouth shut." He shook his head and made a show of fighting against the chains again.

Longarm tapped the knife point against the butt of the Frontier model Colt. "What's the problem, Henry? Think you might've said too much, huh? Sounded to me like you were just gettin' started good. Sure I speak for Marshal Dobbs when I tell you that we wanna know everything. You've already started down the right path. This ain't a good time to quit on us."

Hatchett gazed up at Longarm like a man who'd already been sentenced to a neck-stretching death, the gallows erected, the last meal served, and the end of his time on earth at hand. "You know the kinda horror Lomax is capable of doin', Long. You've seen his handiwork. If the crazy cocksucker so much as suspects what I've said up till now, he'll find me. He'll seek me out, even if'n he has to go all the way to the farthest corner of hell's basement. Soon's I fucked around and opened my mouth, my life wasn't worth a bucket a cold spit."

Longarm could barely contain his surprise when Mason Dobbs darted up and got right in Hatchett's face, shook his finger, and said, "Given all that, you might as well go on ahead and tell us everything you know. Think about it. No point holdin' back now."

Hatchett's gaze darted back and forth between the two lawmen, he sighed, then said, "Got another one of them cheroots, Marshal Long? I sure could use a smoke."

A gun-metal gray cloud hovered between the three men as One-Eyed Henry Hatchett swayed between spilling his guts and not saying another word. After several minutes of stark silence, he grunted. "Shit. I'm a dead man already, I'd wager. Just don't really matter none no how, 'spose. Never shoulda said nothing 'bout any of it to you bastards to begin with."

Barely able to reach the cigar, because of the restrictions to his movement brought on by the chains, Hatchett strained to extract the square-cut stogie from between his lips. Neither lawman offered any assistance as he pushed the smoke into grasping fingers with his tongue, then thumped an inch-and-a-half-long clump of smoldering gray ash onto the floor. At the expense of even more concentrated labor, he was finally able to take another puff, before he groaned, "Well, just fuck me runnin'. Suppose it's a helluva lot better to be a live one-eyed man than a blind dead one."

"Ain't that the way of the world? Now get on with it," Longarm snapped. "The longer you take, the more chance someone else has already died at the blood-soaked hands of Spook Lomax."

"I 'uz tellin' you true back yonder when I said as how I'd only been on two or three of these woman hunts. If memory serves, think this one was my third, or, hell, maybe my fourth. All of 'em took place in and around Trinidad, or hereabouts, leastways. 'Cept for that one down in New Mexico Territory. Ain't ever forgettin' that 'un."

Longarm waved the knife in Hatchett's face. "Quit bobbin' and weavin' on me, and get to the meat of whatever you've got to say."

"Well, I'm just a tryin' to make you understand that it's hard for a man like me to remember all the terrible thangs I've seen, or done. Fact is, rememberin' much of anythang is 'specially hard for a feller when you drink as much whiskey as me and the rest of Spook's gang does most days." He shook his head like a newly saved, penitent sinner. "Takes a got-damn lot of jig juice to drown really awful memories of some of the stuff we've been a part of."

"Jesus," Dobbs said, as he slumped against his own desk and struck a thoughtful pose. "You know, Marshal Long, over the past year we've had at least six women reported missing in and around town. 'Course most of 'em wasn't nothin' but whores. Everyone what knew 'em just figured they'd moved on to the next town. Or that maybe they'd gone on to California, or headed north, or just picked up their meager belongings and left. But, now as I think back on it, there was one or two that didn't fit the alley-bat mold. Merciful Father, we didn't suspect anything like a woman-stealin' ring a operatin' right here in town."

Longarm took a threatening step toward his helpless prisoner but drew up short when the jail's front entrance burst open. The heavy, double-planked wooden door flew back unimpeded and slammed against the wall like a pistol shot.

Dressed in black from head to foot, a woman, nearly six feet tall and strikingly beautiful, stepped across the threshold and headed directly for One-Eyed Henry Hatchett, like someone who definitely meant business.

As though paralyzed by an event that bordered on the impossible to understand, Longarm watched, transfixed, as Hatchett twisted in the chair. The grim-faced female floated into the chained captive's limited view like a shadowy, vengeful angel. A wicked smile flitted across her flawless face.

"Oh, sweet merciful Jesus. You're supposed to be dead," Hatchett groaned, about half a second before the woman fetched out an 1873 model Winchester carbine that she'd carried into the office hidden behind the folds of her split-front riding skirt.

Before Longarm could even think to make a move to

stop it, the black-garbed angel swung the rifle like an ax and whacked Hatchett across the forehead, right above his nose, with the heavy steel barrel.

Longarm couldn't be sure, but he thought he heard the woman hiss, "It's way past time for you to die, you child-killing son of a bitch."

Chapter 9

An involuntary shriek of pain escaped Henry Hatchett's lips when the rifle barrel laid his head open. The surprised outlaw and the dowel-backed seat he was shackled to went over backward in a rush of squawking chair legs and rattling chains. Unconscious, the stunned man's blood-spurting noggin hit the floor hard, bounced, then came to rest at an uncomfortable-looking angle.

Bug-eyed and openmouthed, Mason Dobbs stood rooted behind his battered mahogany desk. The man seemed to be frozen to the floor like a Montana steer caught in a stock-killer of a blue norther, blowing sleet and snow straight down from Canada, all the way to the Texas panhandle.

Hatchett's ruby-lipped attacker's steely-eyed gaze whizzed around the room like the thirty-six-inch log-splitting blade in an Arkansas sawmill. Her cold, focused, blue-eyed stare zeroed in on Longarm, as though challenging him to make any kind of aggressive move in her direction. In spite of himself, his attention got diverted to a pair of partially exposed breasts that rapidly rose and fell beneath a black, lace-front blouse missing its top button.

As much to himself as to anyone else, Longarm mumbled, "My, oh my. Gotta admit, that was one helluva'n entrance, ma'am. Don't by any chance make rabbits appear outta your hat, do you?"

The surprised deputy U.S. marshal watched, dumbfounded, as the woman broke their fleeting eye-to-eye link and expertly jacked a hot round into the short-barreled carbine's well-oiled breech. She brought the stock to her shoulder and took a death-dealing bead on the insensible Hatchett's blood-gusher of a thinker box. Longarm barely managed to leap forward and push the rifle's muzzle harmlessly away before the weapon's thunderous report sent a .45-caliber slug through the Trinidad jail's ceiling and damn near deafened all three conscious occupants of the tiny office.

"Sweet Jesus, girl, what in the hell are you tryin' to do?" he barked—with a considerable expenditure of effort—as he finally wrenched the smoking weapon from the fuming woman's grasp.

Longarm knew without even giving it a second thought that the flush-faced female shooter had not been cowed in the least by his quick response or by the sharply worded questioning of her brutal actions. Much to his added surprise and chagrin, a short-barreled Colt Lightning appeared in her hand. She fired off two shots in Hatchett's general direction before Longarm could respond fast enough to cast the rifle aside and wrestle the pistol away. He was feeling right proud of himself, when the snarling woman slapped him across the face so hard stars the size of wagon wheels formed on the backs of his eyes and floated around the room like gigantic buzzing bees.

Longarm held the flailing, slapping, scratching woman by one wrist, but the instant before he could chuck the pistol into a convenient corner with the rifle, a ten-inch, horn-handled bowie popped up in her free hand, as magically as had the pistol. In spite of his best efforts, and with uncanny accuracy, she expertly tossed the massive knife directly into one of Hatchett's exposed buttocks. The insensate brigand grunted, then made a strangled noise like he'd been kicked by a horse.

Near frantic with the thrashing, whirlwind problem at hand, Longarm was finally able to grab the hellcat by both wrists and call out, "For the sweet love of Jesus, Dobbs, come over here and help me. Good God, don't just stand there like a man that don't know his ass from a water trough. Lend a hand here."

Dobbs shrugged and said, "What the hell am I 'sposed to do?"

"I don't care. Just do somethin'. Anything useful would help for Christ's sake. Gal's wilder'n the worst fuzztail I've ever got a hold of, and she's buckin' in eight different directions at the same time."

Dobbs kept to his spot behind the desk. He held his hands palms up in a feigned posture of terrified submission. "Damned if I will. Angry woman's all yours, Marshal Long. Don't want nothin' to do with fightin' no belligerent females. Whatever you do in a fight with wimmen, you cain't win. You're a loser no matter what the outcome."

With every ounce of muscle left available, Longarm dragged the kicking, screeching example of the fairer sex across the room to the only available empty chair and shoved her into it. He forced her wrists down against the chair's arms. She continued to lash out with booted feet and curse at him. In a final act of desperation, he released one wrist and smacked the heaving woman between the eyes with a two-knuckled blow designed specifically to bring the action to a halt but do a minimal amount of damage. His thrashing opponent went limper than a brush popper's empty leather glove, and her head lolled over to one side.

Near spent from the violent and surprising turn of events, Longarm stood and moved wobble-heeled away from the unmoving female and came to rest leaning against a grinning Mason Dobbs's desk. The raven-haired girl sat slumped in the chair, spraddle-legged, feet propped up on the massive silver rowels of a pair of Mexican spurs, with her head resting on one shoulder.

Longarm snatched two fresh cheroots from his coat pocket, pitched one onto the desk for Dobbs, and lit the other. He shook the smoldering match out, then took a single pull of the rum-soaked tobacco smoke and forced it deep into expectant lungs. He blew a gunmetal blue cloud toward the ceiling, then said, "Well, Dobbs, you gotta admit, that was a bit different."

Around the freshly lit cigar that dangled from the corner of his mouth, Dobbs said, "Yep, I'd say so. Fact is, I ain't never had an armed female bust into my office and try to kill me, or one of my prisoners, before—not ever, as a matter of pure fact. Downright unsettlin', that's what it is, by God. Unsettlin'."

Longarm let out a snort that sounded like an angry bull bison. "Shit, Dobbs, she didn't get anywhere near you. Bet if this fire-breathing gal had started in your direction, you'd be halfway to Boulder right now. Your feet would be smokin' from runnin' so fast, 'cause you'd of already burned the soles off your boots."

Dobbs sounded mighty sure of himself when he shot back, "Knew exactly how to handle the situation, had it been necessary. Just seemed to me as how you had everything under control, and there wasn't any reason for me to get involved or interfere."

A mocking smile etched its way across Longarm's face. "You don't know the lady by any chance, do you?"

Trinidad's city marshal shook his head. "Cain't say as how I've ever seen her before she came through my door ten minutes ago. And just for the record, not sure I'd be callin' this particular female no lady. Any woman as would act the way she just did is pretty much beyond my definition of the word. Hell, I've seen drug-addled whores, out to get money they thought some waddie owed 'em, weren't as hard to get control of as she was."

About then Henry Hatchett stirred and let out a gurgling moan. Longarm wearily moved to the fallen outlaw's side and squatted. He examined the protruding knife's carved-bone handle. "Best leave me the keys to these shackles, then go find your local sawbones and get him over here, Dobbs. I'll jerk this pig-sticker outta Hatchett's perforated rump, 'fore he comes completely around, plug the wound with his kerchief, then drag him back to his cell and lock 'im up."

Dobbs rattled around in a desk drawer till he found a set of keys to the shackles, then ventured an inquisitive but carefully distant stare at the blade jutting from Hatchett's damaged buttock. "How bad is he actually hurt, do you think?"

Longarm coughed out something between a grunt and a snigger. "Well," he said, "it's a sizable hole she put in ole Henry's ass, and likely he's gonna need some serious stitchin' back here. Along with some more up there on his head, where she whacked him with the rifle barrel. There's so much blood all over the poor son of a bitch, it's hard to tell which wound is worse. Think you'd best hurry."

In a matter of minutes, after Dobbs hit the jail's front door running, Longarm had removed Hatchett's shackles, extracted the wide-bladed bowie knife from the wounded man's damaged rump, and had him under lock and key in one of the less than spacious rooms in Trinidad's peckerwood-sized, four-cell lockup. Longarm left the outlaw lying on the floor of the barred stall farthest from the blockhouse door, and made it back to the office just in time to see Hatchett's beautiful attacker come around to something like mushy-headed awareness.

The eye-catching woman leaned forward, elbows on knees, then groggily raised her head and cast a rubbery gaze around the jail, as though trying to determine where she'd landed. She spotted the blood-covered knife on the floor, where Longarm had dropped it. Still appearing slightly muddle-headed, she mumbled, "Is he dead? Did I kill the worthless bag of puss?"

Longarm dragged an empty chair over. He twirled it around, took a seat, pulled his hat off, then leaned on the chair's doweled back so he could comfortably sit facing her. "No, ma'am. He's very much alive, back there in a cell. But, by God, I must admit, you gave sendin' him to Jesus one hell of a try, ma'am. Can't imagine how you missed him twice with the pistol, bein' as you were so close and all. You made some impressive holes in the floor, though."

"Tried my best to ventilate his head."

"Yes, ma'am, that you did. Anyway, sure you'll be pleased to know, Hatchett won't be sittin' proper for some time to come. He'll not ride a horse for quite a spell, and I'd bet goin' to the privy's gonna be a whole new experience for 'im. You put a mighty big hole in his narrow ass with that blade lyin' yonder."

A blue-eyed stare, so cold it came nigh to making Longarm shiver, welded him to his chair. "You can lock that gob of slime away wherever you like, sir. Hide the son of Satan in the deepest mine shaft ever excavated. Shave his head and paint him purple, if you think it'll keep him alive. But I'm here to tell you that, whatever you do, given any possible opportunity I will kill the rotten skunk deader'n a horsefly floatin' in a water trough."

Longarm nodded and tried to give the impression that he understood her unstated motives. "Sure you have your reasons, Miss uhhhh . . . Sorry, but, amidst all the hubbub, I didn't get your name."

"Katarina Thorne. Mrs. Katarina Thorne. Unfortunately, my husband passed nearly six years ago next month, and his untimely death left me a woman alone on a small horse ranch trying to raise an eight-year-old daughter. Buck loved our child more than anything on earth, Marshal. Were he still alive I'm sure he'd be the one sitting here right this very moment. And I'm also absolutely certain you'd be making arrangements to bury that walking stack of cow dung that I could only manage to stick a knife in."

Longarm nodded his respects, then said, "Most pleased to make your acquaintance, Mrs. Thorne. Your obedient servant, Deputy U.S. Marshal Custis Long out of Denver, ma'am. Please forgive me, but I'm bound to ask, what exactly did Hatchett do to incur such murderous feelings on your part?"

Katarina Thorne's determined gaze faltered. She shot a nervous glance around the room, as though trying not to look him in the eye, and finally stared at shaking hands. "Bit over three months ago, he and a group of others, led by a murderer named Spook Lomax, stopped at my ranch on the Canadian River where it joins the Mora, near the tiny community of Wagon Tongue. They surprised and overwhelmed my fourteen-year-old daughter and me. We were alone at the time." Her gaze fell to booted feet. Tears the size of a man's thumb formed at the corners of each eye. "They separated us. That man, Hatchett, led a group that dragged me to the barn. Lomax and some others took Amanda. They savaged the both of us."

Longarm held up a reassuring hand. "You don't have to say any more, Mrs. Thorne."

"Oh, but I do, Marshal Long. When they'd finished with their fun, Amanda had gone to God to be with her father. To this very minute I don't know why, or how, I managed to survive their brutal attack. I suspect that had I been the object of Lomax's attention my life would have been forfeit as well. At any rate, a family friend found me. With his help, I got myself well by gettin' good and mad. We've been chasing those men all over New Mexico Territory and Colorado ever since."

"How'd you find out that I had Henry Hatchett in custody?"

"Oh, that's simple enough. Trailed Lomax and his bunch into town and just listened to all the talk out on Main Street. From what I heard, you're the man who killed Frank McCabe in a local saloon, then brought Hatchett here. Tonight was the first time since the horrible day of Amanda's passing that I've managed to get close enough to any of the Lomax bunch to extract something in the way of *proper* revenge. Was not about to pass up the possibility I might be able to kill one of them."

"You're in pursuit of some mighty dangerous men, Mrs. Thorne. Mighty dangerous."

The icy blue eyes zeroed in on him again. "If there's anyone more aware of that particular fact than me, Marshal Long, then I'd very much like to meet them. Besides, ever since the day of my daughter's death, I've become a mighty dangerous woman myself."

Longarm smiled. "Well, I think perhaps I can help put your mind at ease, Mrs. Thorne. You see, my sole purpose for being in Trinidad is to find Spook Lomax and make certain he never hurts anyone like you, or your daughter, again."

Katarina Thorne's focus sharpened and she leaned forward and displayed a look of considerably more interest. "Well, you're just a bit late. Lomax and a number of his soulless minions have, by all evidence, already fled the area. But, you know, Marshal, I think we could be a great deal of help to you in any effort to bring Lomax to justice."

Quizzical interest flashed across Longarm's face. " 'We'? What do you mean, 'we'?"

The jailhouse door burst open again. The thick slab of iron-bound timbers hit the wall and bounced back like a clap of thunder. Longarm snapped a glance over Katarina Thorne's shoulder just in time to gaze down the gaping muzzle of a ten-gauge shotgun. The monstrous blaster rested in the hands of a gigantic man, who bore more than a passing resemblance to an angry Rocky Mountain grizzly. Near seven feet tall and heavily bearded, he was covered in a variety of tanned and layered hides. Whatever else lay beneath that pile of skins was barely discernable, except for the carved-ivory stump that protruded from the place where one of his legs once resided.

From deep inside the man's chest came the distinct sound of an atavistic growl. "Thought I done tole you to wait for me, Kate." The bearlike figure took a single, floor-thumping step forward, stopped, and quickly flicked an all-encompassing glance around the office. "Keep yore hands on the chair back, mister. Make any sudden moves and I'll splatter yew all over hell and half-a-Sunday." His slit-eyed, animalistic gaze bored its way into Longarm like a twisted drill bit. "This goober eater the only one around, Kate?"

Katarina Thorne's eyes never left Longarm. Once again, a confident, self-assured smile spread across her handsome face. "Yes, he's alone, Night. This is what I meant by 'we,' Marshal Long. Please say a friendly hello to a devoted old acquaintance and ally of the family's, Orpheus Nightshade—a lifelong friend of my dead husband's. Mr. Nightshade is the family friend I mentioned who found me after the Lomax gang killed my daughter and left me for dead."

Chapter 10

Longarm offered up an uncomfortable nod. Orpheus Nightshade nodded back, but didn't lower the .10-gauge blaster—not so much as a fraction of an inch.

The enormous creature tilted his head toward the woman and snarled, "You kill tother'n, Kate? That Hatchett maggot good and dead yet?"

Katarina Thorne stood, strode majestically to the knife on the floor, bent over, and snatched it up. She wiped the bloody, razor-sharp blade on her skirt and shoved it into a pressed-leather, metal-lined sheath hanging from the pistol belt beneath her coat. With a loud *click*, the weapon snapped into place and once again vanished amid the various folds and layers of her dark-colored clothing.

Hands fisted on shapely hips, she turned and faced Longarm and her oversized friend. "No, the good marshal here wouldn't let me finish the skunk off, Night. 'Course I tried. Feel as though I gave it a pretty good effort. And I did put a nick or two in Hatchett's more than worthless hide. He won't be forgetting me anytime soon."

Nightshade made a noise like he'd just come out of hibernation. "Where's Hatchett now? We need him to tell us again that which we already suspect, don't yew think?"

With the same sense of purpose and power that exuded

from her every move, the Thorne woman quickly marched over to the corner where her carbine and pistol littered the dusty floor. Once re-armed, she reclaimed the chair directly in front of Longarm's seat, laid the rifle across her lap, then leaned over so her face was within inches of the lawman's. He could easily see the tense lines around her eyes.

"We're pretty sure we know where Spook Lomax is headed from Trinidad, Marshal Long. We've chased him from the Cornudo Hills of New Mexico Territory, to Cheyenne Wells, Colorado—where his gang murdered five people—back down to the North Canadian near Seneca, and then, in a roundabout way to here. Talked with a lot of people he abused along the way. What we need now is confirmation. Henry Hatchett can give us that."

Nightshade puffed up. "Con-fir-mation. That's the word, by God. Con-fir-mation."

Longarm let one corner of his mouth creak its way into a half smile. "Well, you're welcome to try. He's back yonder in the corner cell. Doubt you'll get much out of him though, Mrs. Thorne. He's tougher'n a hard-boiled boot heel."

With Longarm locked in her frosty gaze, she tilted her ebony-haired head slightly and said, "Mr. Nightshade, do you think Henry Hatchett will tell us where Spook Lomax is headed?"

Chapped lips peeled away from Orpheus Nightshade's pointed, canine teeth. An unclipped, droopy moustache brushed his tongue as he spoke. "Oh, you let me have 'im for just about two minutes, Kate. Garn-tee he'll tell us anything you ever wanted to hear about ole Spook Lowmax. He'll bawl like a baby, dance like a monkey on a string, and give up tales of all his own earthly sins against man-

and womankind—along with anything else he ever knew. Sure as one of them Catholic folks a goin' to confession. Jus' like that evil skunk we talked with down in New Mexico Territory two weeks ago at Arroyo Christobal, what tole us as how his boss wuz a comin' up here to Trinidad."

Mildly surprised at the pair's deadly determination, Longarm said, "You talked to one of Lomax's men two weeks ago?"

Kate Thorne leaned back in the uncomfortable wooden seat and appeared to relax. She crossed her arms over her chest, thereby blocking Longarm's nearly unfettered view of her ample bosom. "Well, truth be told, we did most of the talking, Marshal Long. He was a wounded straggler from Spook's gang, name of Bucky Smoot. I recognized him as one of the men who accompanied Lomax, when the gang raided my ranch."

Longarm squirmed in his chair. "So the two of you had a come-to-Jesus meeting with Bucky Smoot?"

Orpheus Nightshade jumped in. "Near as we could tell from the way he acted, poor ole broke-legged Bucky wanted nothing more than to unburden his immortal soul 'fore he met up with the maker. Man confessed to a whole passel of horrible behavior. Sins of the most shockin' kind. Hell, he cried, told us plenty, and then he up and, all of a sudden like, keeled over stone-cold dead. Coulda been the bullet I put in his head, I suppose. But then again, guess it coulda been a heart attack, or maybe a killer strain of the gout. He had the look of the type who'd have a death-dealin' heart attack to me."

Longarm started to reach for a cheroot, glanced at the shotgun pointed at his head, and thought better of it. "Did poor ole sin-burdened Bucky Smoot say how he got himself hurt?"

"Stupid bastard got drunk and fell off his horse," Nightshade snorted. "Broke his fool leg. Bad for him. Good for us. Didn't take much in the way of pressure applied to that break and he spilled his guts faster'n the flames of hell can scorch a sinner's coattail. Said the Lomax bunch wuz a headed straight for all the pleasure afforded by Trinidad's palaces of worldly delights. 'Pears as how he went and tole us the truth, don't it?"

Kate Thorne flipped the saddle ring back and forth on the carbine with her finger. "Unfortunately," she said, "he died right after telling us where the Lomax gang might be headed after their visit to Trinidad, Marshal. Thought sure we'd be able to catch up with the whole bunch here, but they're gone now. And that's why we're here to talk with Hatchett."

"You folks mind if I smoke?" Longarm asked and made a nonthreatening motion toward his vest pocket.

A broad smile spread over Kate Thorne's face. "Not at all, Marshal. Please, go right ahead and have your cigar." She waved a dismissive hand at her enormous protector. "You can lower the shotgun, Night. I don't believe Marshal Long intends us any harm."

Nightshade let the hammers down on the .10-gauge blaster, then swung it around to hang on his shoulder from a leather strap attached to the weapon by metal swivels. He stood rigidly erect, like a peg-legged soldier at military attention. "Well, she's down, Kate." He patted the weapon's oiled stock. "But don't you be forgettin' 'bout Mae Belle, mister. She can come back up for action mighty damned quick. Should she have to speak at this distance they won't be enough of you left to fill a thimble."

Longarm gingerly eased two fingers into his vest pocket and lifted a cheroot out. "Oh, don't you worry, Mr. Nightshade. I'm not about to forget about Mae Belle." He fired the smoke, took a much needed puff, then said, "Now, then, just where do you think Lomax is headed, Kate? Oh, do you mind if I call you Kate?"

A wicked grin flitted across Katarina Thorne's crimson lips. "We're not exactly friends—yet—Marshal Long, but with stilted social custom put aside, I don't mind if you call me Kate. Practically everyone does."

"Good, very good. And I'd be most pleased if you'd agree to call me Custis."

"Of course you would. Not sure I can, but I'll certainly try."

Longarm blew smoke at the ceiling, then said, "Now back to the question at hand. Where do you good folks think Lomax is headed?"

Kate flicked at something unseen on the front of her skirt. "No *thinkin'* involved. Given what Bucky Smoot told us, under extreme duress I might add, we're pretty sure we know exactly where Lomax and his pack of killers are headed from here. But, in spite of our rapidly developing friendship, Custis, I'm not about to tell you another thing until I have your personal guarantee that Mr. Nightshade and I can accompany any posse sent out after them."

"Oh, there won't be any posse, Kate. Just me."

Nightshade snorted, then coughed into his hand. "That might well be the funniest thing I've heard a grown man say in years, or the stupidest. Hard to tell. Difficult to measure stupid."

Longarm thumped ash from his cheroot, cast an irritated glance at Kate Thorne's guardian angel, then arched an eyebrow. Something of a sneer crept into his voice when he said, "How so, Orpheus?"

The big man broke out of his rigid stance, thumped over

to Marshal Dobbs's desk on his carved-ivory leg, and sat down on one corner. He leaned over and placed a plate-sized hand on Longarm's shoulder. "'Cause you've no idea, as yet, where we're headed, me tiny, little boyo."

Longarm's head snapped around as the jailhouse door slowly creaked open. Nightshade came to his one good foot like a wary, half-starved tomcat and brought the shotgun around for possible business.

Mason Dobbs eased his head into the room through the opening, then glanced around like a lost goose. Big eyes got even bigger when he spotted Orpheus Nightshade, but he nerved up enough to step inside, then made an almost imperceptible flicking motion with one hand at someone who'd followed him.

A short, thin, hawk-faced man, who wore wire-rimmed spectacles low on his nose and carried a battered, leather bag, maneuvered his way through the tiny opening and around Dobbs. He tipped his black, short-brimmed hat, and in a tone that commanded attention snapped, "Dr. Eli Winterborne at your service, Marshal, ma'am. You have a wounded man here, I'm told. Knifed in one buttock, as I understand it."

Longarm hooked a thumb toward the jail's lockup. "He's back yonder, Doc. Patched him up, as best I could. Think I stopped most of the bleedin'. But he's probably gonna need some needlework done on the hole in his bony rump."

"We'll see," Winterborne said as he disappeared through the doorway leading into the cellblock.

Behind an amused grin, Longarm watched Mason Dobbs make his jittery way around Orpheus Nightshade to his chair behind the desk. Trinidad's city marshal moved like he'd just discovered the biggest rattlesnake in Colorado lying in the middle of the floor of his house. Night-shade returned the favor by eyeing Dobbs as though he'd spotted a tiny, insignificant dung beetle he might enjoy squashing at the first opportunity.

"Now," Longarm said, "let's get back to our discussion, Kate. Terribly sorry, but I can't take either of you with me on any hunt for Spook Lomax and his bunch of killers."

She cast a benevolent smile his way and said, "In that case, Custis, we can't tell you where he's headed. Or maybe I should say, we won't tell you."

As Longarm raised his finger and was about to start in on a heartfelt lecture listing the dangers of the trail, the uncertainty of such endeavors, and the very real possibility of imminent, violent death, Henry Hatchett cut loose with a series of gut-wrenching, staccato squeals. Then the poor stabbed-in-the-ass fool painted the air blue with loud, detailed curses that shot from the deepest reaches of the cellblock and assaulted the eardrums of everyone in the outer office.

Kate Thorne waved Longarm into silence, then said, "I've already heard all the objections to my participation in this venture you could possibly raise, Custis. Orpheus hits me almost hourly with at least half a dozen reasons why I shouldn't be on this manhunt. I'll not hear any such talk from someone I barely know. The deal stands as offered. You will let us talk to Hatchett. If he confirms what we already believe, then, and only then, you can accompany us as we continue on with our search for the murderous skunk."

Longarm came out of his chair and was just before giving the dark-eyed beauty a real dressing-down, when Doc Winterborne strolled from the cellblock, bloody hands extended, and hustled over to the washstand near the front door.

Everyone watched in silence, as the gore-stained pill roller poured water into the basin, then rinsed his hands and arms all the way up to his elbows. While drying himself he said, "Well, I did the best I could, folks. Boiled that hole in his ass out with carbolic. Stitched it up. He'd best be prayin' it don't fester. Head wound was considerably larger—messy business. Bled all over the damned place. Gonna leave one hellacious ugly scar. Man's gonna have one damnable bad headache for a few days, and I doubt he'll be able to sit on that knife wound for at least a week or two, maybe longer." He pitched the stained towel onto the washstand, then pushed his sleeves back down and buttoned them.

"Can we talk to him, Doctor?" Kate asked.

"Don't see why not. But you'd best do it now. Once he gets some of these pills in him that I'm gonna leave to help with the pain, doubt he'll be able to stay awake. And even if you could rouse him, doubt he'd make much sense."

Dobbs hustled over and helped Winterborne get back into his threadbare suit jacket. "I'll just walk Doc back to his office," he said. "You folks go right on ahead and have your talk with One-Eyed Henry Hatchett. I'd appreciate it if you'd get the deed done 'fore I come back."

Longarm started for the cellblock door, but Nightshade pushed him aside with one enormous arm and motioned Kate Thorne in first. Longarm was forced to wait even longer, while the woman's enormous protector maneuvered his massive bulk through the same opening and eventually inside the tiny cell. Longarm could sense an air of tense expectation oozing off both of them.

Chapter 11

Henry Hatchett lay sprawled on his stomach atop a corn-shuck mattress that spilled over the sides of a wooden bunk made from rough-cut pine planks. His semibare, now bandaged behind poked from the folds of a ratty blanket like a pale, fleshy moon rising over wintry Rockies. A kerosene lamp flickered from the seat of a stool in the corner and bathed the entire area in the sickly yellow hue brought on by a badly adjusted wick.

By the time Longarm finally negotiated his way inside the cramped jail cell with the others, Orpheus Nightshade was more than ready to start the questioning. Kate nodded and the moose-sized man whipped out a Texas bowie with a thirteen-and-a-half-inch blade that was as broad as a man's hand. The weapon looked remarkably like a bone-handled meat cleaver. He leaned over the wounded Hatchett and swatted the brigand on the damaged and recently bandaged part of his rump with the flat side of the gigantic piece of razor-sharp steel. The distinct, slapping noise of metal against flesh caused Longarm to wince.

Hatchett made a sound that would have had the power to jerk tears out of a glass eye, if anyone who really cared had been present.

Kate bent over so her lips were near the weeping man's

ear. She almost whispered, "My extremely large friend and I are only gonna ask you this question once, mister. Where is Spook Lomax headed from Trinidad?"

"Jesus," Hatchett whined through the river of tears streaming down his contorted face.

"Wrong answer," Nightshade snapped, then swatted Hatchett's recently repaired ass again.

The wounded outlaw shot a pained, wide-eyed glance at his tormentors and screeched like a stomped cat. "Shit and goddamn," he yelped. "For the love of Jesus, don't hit me anymore. Hell, I'll tell you whatever you want to know, just don't go whackin' my butchered-up ass with that damned knife again."

Nightshade turned to Longarm and grinned down at him. "See. Told you he'd talk, didn't I?"

Kate leaned closer the second time. Her voice was barely a whisper. "Best get it right this time, Henry. Mr. Nightshade gets right testy if he has to do the same thing more than twice. Where's Lomax headed?"

Between liquid gasps, Hatchett managed to gurgle, "Raton. He's goin' down to Raton, and then on to Black Mesa. He's headed for Black Mesa, I swear it. Been workin' outta Black Mesa for years. Now, for the love of God, you crazy bitch, leave me the hell alone. I'm in a hellacious lot of pain."

Kate Thorne immediately came back to her full height. "Finally. Now that's the right answer." Longarm watched as the woman's face hardened into a frigid, tight-lipped mask. Her eyes narrowed up on the injured brigand like the adjustable peep sights on a Sharps buffalo rifle. "And don't worry," she cooed in a quiet, soothing voice, as though speaking to a child. "You won't be feeling any more pain, you child-killing son of a bitch."

112

A tiny, two-shot derringer flashed into Kate Thorne's rock-steady hand.

Too late, Longarm realized what was about to occur. "Damn, girl, how many guns are you carryin'?" He tried to reach across Orpheus Nightshade and slap the pistol aside, but Kate's determined defender grabbed the lawman's flailing arm, leaned his enormous bulk against the stunned marshal, and pinned him against the bars like a steer in a cattle chute. Then the monster threw a tree trunk–sized forearm across his trapped victim's throat. Grinning, he held Longarm there as though toying with a small child.

Each time Custis Long tried for one of his pistols, Nightshade slapped his hand away and laughed. Unable to do anything to stop it, he could only watch as the fiery-eyed woman kneeled, placed the derringer's muzzle directly against Henry Hatchett's temple, and pulled the trigger.

The outlaw barely twitched when the slug bored through his skull and rocked his head sideways across the shuck mattress. A perfectly shaped hole opened a finger-sized floodgate of hot, dark blood that spewed out in a steady stream like beer from a barrel's open bunghole.

Nearly unable to breathe, Longarm gurgled, "Sweet Jesus, Kate." Then he abandoned the struggle and leaned limply against the bars like a wet rag.

The Thorne woman rose, dropped the palm-sized pistol on the floor beside Hatchett's bunk, then turned and pushed on Orpheus Nightshade until she could get her face to a spot a few inches away from Longarm's. Flushed and obviously growing angrier by the second, she stared directly into the lawman's eyes, pointed toward the corpse, and said, "That sorry sack of animal waste helped despoil and murder my fourteen-year-old virginal daughter."

"Trust me, I understand," Longarm grunted.

A single tear the size of a man's thumb rolled down Kate's cheek, then dropped onto the sleeve of Longarm's coat. "I swore on her pitiful grave I would kill him and all the others who took part in that shameful deed. That's exactly what I intend to do. Kill 'em all."

"Oh, I believe you now. Yessir, I believe."

"There's not a jury in the West that will convict me for taking his sorry life, Marshal Long. Did you really think for a single instant that I would leave this place and let him stay alive?"

Longarm pulled on Nightshade's forearm in an effort to get it off his throat so he could speak freely. He coughed, spit, then said, "Well, Kate, sure as hell didn't think you'd kill 'im right here in front of me. 'Course, I guess that's a pretty short-sighted assumption on my part, bein' as how you'd already tried to rub him out several times earlier this evening while I watched."

Nightshade cackled like a thing insane, then snorted, "By God, looks to me like the son of a bitch went and kilt hisself, lawdog. Seemed right depressed to me. Probably couldn't stand the pain from his wounds. Big ole extra hole in yore ass like that 'un has gotta hurt somethin' terrible."

Longarm rolled his eyes. "Yeah, I suppose."

"Or maybe he was just so 'shamed of all the horrible crimes he'd done committed over the years, he just found it impossible to face life amongst good folk for a single minute longer. 'Sides, should anyone ask, I'll swear Kate was in the outer office, and I seen him pull the trigger my very own self. Tried like hell to stop the sad deed, but he was one determined bad man."

"We're going to that rat's nest, Raton. Then, on to Black Mesa if necessary, Custis," Kate said. "And we're leaving right now. You can either go with us, or, as God as my wit-

114

ness, I'll have Mr. Nightshade crack your neck like a chicken bone. Not you or anyone else will keep me from my appointment with the bloody vengeance I intend to visit on Lomax. So, what's it gonna be, Marshal? Speak right up."

Longarm flinched like Nightshade's Mae Belle had just gone off in his face. "You've no idea what you're talking about, Kate. Raton's worse than Trinidad. Ever since the railroad started over the pass, the town's gone from a sleepy little New Mexican village to bein' a small-time version of Sodom and Gomorrah. Damned little, if any, law. And Black Mesa's as bad an area for killers and thieves as it gets. It's a snake pit way the hell over on the edge of Cherokee Outlet. We could have talked all night long and not mentioned that godless place."

"You didn't answer the lady's question, lawdog," Nightshade grunted. "Jes' gimme the word, Kate. I'll disjoint this jaybird like a pullet we're gonna fry up for supper."

Katarina Thorne placed a quieting hand on the powerful arm draped across Longarm's windpipe. "We're gonna need him, Night. Most likely gonna need 'im real bad before this whole mess all shakes out. The local lawman, Dobbs, is obviously about as worthless as a screen door in an outhouse. No one else around Trinidad's gonna help people like us. Folk they don't know from scarlet Judas—especially if we're asking them to help us confront a murderer like Spook Lomax."

Nightshade got nose to nose with Longarm. "Want me to take all these pistols he's a carryin' away from 'im, Kate?"

"Ah, not a good idea to go unarmed in a place like Raton. No, that shouldn't be necessary, Night. Should it, Marshal Long?"

"Absolutely not," Longarm shot back. If there's one thing he didn't need, he thought, it was to be totally defenseless right then.

"He'll most likely need all his weapons—and more—when we get over the pass. You know he's right. Raton is worse than Trinidad, and from what we've heard, almost as bad as Black Mesa."

"I let you go, you gonna behave, mister?" Nightshade snarled.

Longarm tried to suck some air past his compressed windpipe and into starving lungs, then grunted, "Hell, yes, I'll behave. Just get off me, you big son of a bitch. Can't breathe worth a damn with you a leanin' on me like this."

Nightshade backed away, but brought the shotgun up again for quick use. He glowered at Longarm, then said, "I'm a watchin' you, mister. Don't go and try nothin' real stupid."

A look of studied concern settled on Kate Thorne's face as she watched Longarm paw at his abused throat. "Are you gonna be all right, Marshal Long?"

"Yeah," Longarm muttered. "Just have to get a tablespoon or so of fresh air into my lungs. Feel like I've been run over by a fully loaded Denver and Rio Grande freight. Jesus, how much do you weigh, Orpheus?"

"What the hell's my weight got to do with anything?" the big man grumped.

"Just askin', that's all. Don't go to bellerin' and pawin' at the ground."

"You tryin' to insult me, you tiny little pimple? How 'bout if'n I step on yore head and render it out for squz?"

Longarm stretched, then patted himself as if to check for the possibility of broken bones. "Calm down. Just talkin' to make sure I still can. Hell, thought for a minute or

116

two you were gonna turn all the bones in my throat into powder."

A look of mild confusion flitted across Nightshade's hair-covered face. He wagged his head like a stray dog looking for a handout. "'Bout three fifty, last time I got on a cattle scale."

"Three hundred and fifty pounds? God Almighty, wonder you didn't squish me like a fly."

"That's enough," Kate snapped. "Let's get out of here before Dobbs comes back. Do you have a horse, Marshal?"

"Hell, no. Didn't arrive in town till late this afternoon. Haven't had time to even think about it. Must be near midnight now. Doubt I'll be able to rent one this late."

"Doesn't matter," Kate said over her shoulder as she stomped out of the cellblock and headed for the front door. "We have an extra animal you can ride. Big *gruello* gelding named Booger. You're gonna love him. Bet the two of you'll get along just fine. But you'd best be aware, he's a biter. Saw him take a man's finger off once."

Chapter 12

A glacial moon the color of frozen silver and the size of a dinner plate turned night into day each time it peeked from behind dense, roiling clouds that spit ice-tinged rain onto the road from Trinidad to Raton. Heavy lids scratched their way across Longarm's tired eyes. While accustomed to lengthy periods on the trail with little rest, the train trip from Denver and the long, troubled day in Trinidad had begun to take their toll. He pulled his collar and scarf up around cold ears, then glanced heavenward and said a silent, "Thank you, Jesus," that Nightshade and Kate had waited long enough for him to retrieve his heavy canvas coat, gloves, and other necessaries from the Armijo.

In need of sleep, Longarm swayed in the saddle as he followed along behind Kate Thorne. The California-style saddle on Kate's snappish, line-backed dun had turned out to be a very comfortable seat for a midnight run. So comfortable, in fact, he was having trouble keeping himself awake.

Several hundred feet ahead, Orpheus Nightshade led the party along the broad, well-kept road that would eventually lead up the slope of the Raton Pass to its 7800-foot summit before falling again into New Mexico Territory. Longarm's mind sharpened when he noticed that Nightshade had suddenly come to a dead stop. The man had removed his hat, and his enormous head was tilted to one side, as though he listened for something in the dark distance.

Kate Thorne reined up on one side of the bearded giant, Longarm on the other.

Kate gazed up at her friend and said, "Why're we stopping, Night? What's the problem?"

The mountain man tilted his head and cupped an ear. To Longarm the man looked like a dog patiently listening to its owner talk nonsense. "Quiet, Kate. Listen, just listen," Nightshade whispered.

After several seconds, Longarm said, "What're we listenin' for? Nothin' but the blowin' wind a gettin' to my ears."

He was barely able to hear the man speak when Nightshade breathed, "Give it a chance, Marshal. It'll come."

All of a sudden, Longarm's skin prickled, and bumpy, cold, chicken flesh crawled up his back. Sweeping down from the foothills of the Sangre de Cristo Mountains a freshening wind knifed through the layers of leather and cloth between his skin and the cold. Out of the darkness of the tree line nearly a mile away, the blustering currents of ice-tinged air carried the barely audible sound of a strangled, trilling cry. A faint, high-pitched shriek of weeping agony so reedlike, as to sound almost like gusting air passing over a stretch of frozen barbed wire. The agony, borne on the wind, twisted its way into his very soul. Distant and faint, the pained wail rose and fell like soul-rending music. Then the spine-chilling silence flooded back.

"Probably nothin' more'n the wind," Longarm offered. "If not, it could well be coming from miles away."

"No," Nightshade said, pointing a glove-covered finger the size of a hammer handle north by west. "They's a ranch house over yonder way. I seen the smoke from the place when me'n Kate was headed for Trinidad two days ago. Big corral. Barn. Adobe shack. Looked like a small horse-raisin' operation."

The skin-tingling cry crept up out of the nighttime gloom again. It hit Longarm's ears like a slow-moving wave lapping at the bank of a frozen lake. Louder the second time. More unnerving.

Kate's long-legged, black mare stamped one foot and shook its head, then shifted from one back foot to the other. She reached out and patted the animal's neck, then turned, reached up, and placed the same hand on her friend's arm. "What do you think it is, Night?"

"No need fer me to think on it much, Kate. Sounds an awful lot like a woman—a woman in unbearable pain. Most like a soul lost in the deepest recesses of Satan's burnin' lake of fire. Gives me the quiverin' willies just to hear such a gut-wrenchin' cry."

Longarm leaned on the tall, slender horn of his borrowed saddle. "Not gettin' anything done sittin' here, folks. If you're of a mind to, why don't we go see what's about? Knowin' Spook Lomax and his bunch are in the area, I just couldn't live with myself if I rode away. The thought that I might have left an injured woman in need of help to the vagaries of chance, or the further ministrations of Lomax, is repugnant to me in the extreme."

The shrill wail rose on the wind and became even more piercing to the ear and heart. Now and again the entire murky night was brightened for a few dazzling seconds by the brilliant *luna de la plata*, as it blazed through random holes in the gunpowder-colored clouds overhead. In an isolated shaft of moonlight, Kate appeared to tremble. She turned away from Nightshade and stared into the

121

darkness and gloom, as though searching for the howler's inky origins.

"I agree with Marshal Long, Night," Kate said, slapping her reins against one gloved palm. "Can't begin to imagine leaving this place until we all know what has transpired with whoever is making such a heartrending sound."

"How far away is she, Orpheus?" Longarm's quiet question appeared directed as much at the wind as to Kate Thorne's guardian.

Nightshade sounded distant, distracted, when he muttered, "A mile. Maybe even a bit less."

Longarm flipped his reins toward the tree-covered hills. "Well, lead on, big boy. We ain't gonna get nothin' much done sittin' here with our ears cocked against this skin-numbin' wind."

Longarm and Kate urged their animals forward as Nightshade led the way through a jumbled patch of jagged boulders scattered along the side of the road, then across a wide strip of bone-dry, brittle grass. The frozen weeds grew belly high on the horses and made glassy, clicking sounds as they passed. After a few minutes Nightshade turned almost due north and headed toward a newly revealed pinpoint of light at the edge of the distant tree line.

Twenty minutes later the wary party descended into a sheltered cup of land, where they drew their animals to a halt near a split-rail fence. Rough wooden railings surrounded an empty corral space. The trio dismounted under a leafless, umbrella-shaped oak, located some twenty to thirty yards distance from a squatty, windowless adobe house. A dim light flickered inside the silent structure and could be seen flowing from the open doorway like a luminous liquid someone had accidentally spilled across the rugged threshold. Longarm thought it more than a bit suspicious that no horses were anywhere in evidence.

The eerie wailing from inside the block-shaped house had diminished as Longarm and his cohorts drew ever nearer. A low-throated moan, a sound they'd been unable to detect from the Raton road, replaced the high-pitched crying and further added to the already sinister sensations created by the seemingly deserted dwelling.

Nightshade handed his reins to Kate, limbered up the .10 gauge, then whispered, "Stay with the horses. Me'n this here Denver lawdog'll stroll over and see what's goin' on."

Kate snatched at her friend's sleeve. "I won't," she hissed. "God only knows who, or what, might be hiding in the shadows just waiting for you to walk away and leave me alone."

Longarm pulled both hip pistols and cocked them, then stepped closer to his agitated companions. "Best if you do as he says, Kate—leastways until we can determine what we're confronted with. Besides, way I figure it, as many weapons as a nervy woman like you carries, the proper attitude would be to feel right sorry for any brigand as might think himself bold enough to happen on you in the dark."

"Oh, that's rich," she snorted, then turned and slipped the Winchester from its hand-tooled boot. "All right," she said and jacked a shell into the chamber. "I'll stand over there in the shadows beside the oak."

"Sounds good to me. But if that's where you're gonna go, don't be movin' around until we call for you. Could be might dangerous if you do," Longarm said.

"Well, if anything goes amiss, boys, you can expect me to come heeling it your direction as fast as I can run, dangerous or not. Anything I see that doesn't appear to belong is going to get shot dead and right damned quick."

Longarm watched the audacious woman silently blend in with the shadowy dimness at the base of the enormous tree. As he turned back toward Kate's overly protective companion, Nightshade silently motioned for him to move around on the right of the ranch house's open entrance.

Pistols at the ready, Longarm crept across the grassless yard, then turned for the building itself and whatever horror lay inside. He tried to match his movements, step for step, with those of Orpheus Nightshade. They arrived on opposite ends of the cabin's rough plank veranda at the same time, then quietly stepped onto the dilapidated porch and plastered themselves against an unpainted wall peppered with the deep pockmarks left by hundreds of bullets.

The strange moaning stopped as soon as Longarm's foot hit the dusty porch. Hidden by dense shadows near the door, a dog that looked amazingly like a full-grown wolf the size of a small pony slowly came to its feet. Hackles raised to the maximum, it growled, then limped several wobbly steps in his direction. As the beast moved into the light, Longarm heard Nightshade make a low clucking sound. The creature stopped and turned completely around in its tracks. Amazingly, a few seconds later, the growling stopped, and Longarm could see the animal's ragged tail wag back and forth, as though it had come upon a long-lost friend.

With as much stealth as he could muster, Longarm slipped to the open doorway and peeked inside. Nightshade continued to work at occupying the home's obviously wounded guardian.

The entire front portion of the home's interior was a single large room lighted by a dying kerosene lantern—a busy space where each corner had been fitted for its distinct and particular purpose. One area, just inside the door, served for receptions. Adjacent to it, another section was dressed out for relaxation. There was a portion where a man might sit down for meals, and another, curtained off with a blanket, where the occupants probably slept at night—all neat, tidy, and apparently once could have been considered well-kept.

Longarm glanced down at the threshold, looking for a solid spot to place his foot. Pools of gore splattered the puncheon floor. Drag marks in the sticky, near-dried blood led from the threshold to a spot directly in front of a rock fireplace, located in the cabin's back wall and equipped for cooking. A motionless woman sat on the floor, her back propped against the raised stone hearth. The blood-drenched corpse of a man lay next to her, his head resting in her saturated lap.

Longarm stepped inside the silent room and pushed the double-thick plank door completely open, as he glanced from corner to corner. A board under one foot groaned and the woman's wispy-haired head snapped up.

A screech that sounded as though it came from someplace on the other side of hell rose from her thin chest. A Colt pistol appeared in a hand that dripped blood. Her thunderous first shot drowned out the screaming. The heavy .45-caliber slug hit the door frame within inches of Longarm's head. He dropped to the floor as the second deafening blast sent a blue whistler through the spot in the air where his heart had just been.

Damned woman's a helluva good shot, he thought, then rolled to his right as quickly as he could, as a third and forth shot nicked the floorboards where he passed. With a loud *click*, her fifth effort landed on a dead chamber—as did the sixth.

Longarm leapt to his feet, holstered his pistols, rushed

the distraught woman, and attempted to snatch the weapon from her hand, as she tried to insert the barrel into her own mouth.

"No, no, please God, no," he said, as he knelt beside the blood-coverd female and pried the still-smoking gun from her hand. "I mean you no harm, missus. I came to help you." He placed a reassuring hand on the distraught woman's shoulder, but her agitated eyes darted toward the doorway, and when her gaze fell on Orpheus Nightshade, she screamed like a gut-shot panther again.

Longarm motioned the huge man back outside and yelled, "Get Kate in here, Nightshade. Do it now."

For some seconds the screeching continued, but as soon as Kate Thorne's open, friendly smile appeared next to Longarm's, the woman calmed dramatically. In short order they disentangled her from the head-shot corpse and assisted her unsteady move to a chair at the kitchen table. Longarm stood aside and watched as Kate worked to further soothe the blood-covered female.

After the passage of several minutes, during which time Longarm worked to make a pot of coffee, Kate called the marshal back to the table. "Custis, this is Miriam Westbrook. That's her husband there by the fireplace. His name was Donald. Miriam, I want you to tell the marshal the same thing you just told me."

Trembling, bony hands the color of rust rose to Miriam Westbrook's haggard, waxen face. Years of hard work and constant trepidation had chiseled away at her once good looks. All of a sudden, she noticed the dried blood on her fingers and appeared about to come unhinged again. Longarm quickly took a seat at the table, then leaned forward and said, "We'll help you get the blood off, Mrs. Westbrook. All it will take is a bit of water."

Kate cooed, "Please, Miriam. Take your time. Repeat the story you just told me. Marshal Long needs to hear it. He needs to hear it all directly from your lips."

The Westbrook woman's wild-eyed gaze rarely left her own hands. She placed them on the table in front of her, and only looked up in nervous, darting glances. In a flat, frozen, emotionless voice, she said, "Earlier this evenin', long 'fore it got dark, men came. Musta been close on to a dozen of 'em. Frightenin'-lookin' men they wuz. Killers and thieves, beyond any doubt. Worst of all, their leader had the look of a haint—a dead man ridin' a horse. I'd never seen such a man, 'cept maybe in a coffin. But I swear 'fore Jesus, I seen him my very own self." Longarm strained to hear her speak.

She broke off and appeared to withdraw for some moments. Kate patted one of the bloodied hands. "Take your time, Miriam. Take your time. Marshal Long must hear the whole story."

Tears streamed down Miriam Westbrook's face as she struggled to continue. "W-w-we've been here a l-l-long time, you see. My husband was always s-s-suspicious of those who stopped by uninvited. We're so close to the road now, you know. Lots of bad people on the road these days. Not as safe as when we arrived here thirty year ago. That's why there ain't no windows in the house. Only gun slots. We've had to fight off bands of brigands a number of times over the years. None like these men, though. None like them."

Longarm tried his best to speak in as soothing a manner as possible when he said, "Mrs. Westbrook, I know this is going to be a difficult matter for you. But you must tell me, how did your husband die?"

Bloodshot eyes darted toward the front door. "We seen

'em comin'. Bunch of 'em. Donald said it best we get inside and fort up. The ghost walked right up on the porch after we got inside. My husband talked to him through the slot in that door yonder. But when Donald refused to open up, the phantom pushed a pistol barrel through the gun slot and shot him in the head before he even had time to think. I couldn't believe what had happened. When Donald fell, I knew I'd have to fight 'em, or they'd surely kill me as well, or somethin' worse. So I fought 'em, tooth and nail."

Longarm leaned back in his chair. "You alone drove the Lomax gang off?"

Sounding as if she spoke from the bottom of a deep pit, she said, "Was at the gun port next to the door when Donald went down from bein' shot by the ghost. Fired at least three shots directly into the pasty-faced specter what kilt him. Must've passed right through. Didn't appear to even slow the monster down."

Longarm shook his head and muttered, "Know exactly what you mean, Mrs. Westbrook. I've seen that particular bit of magic myself."

"Couldn't believe my amazed eyes. Pale-skinned and red-eyed, he turned in a flurry of trailing cloth and ran from the porch to his waiting horse and men. I fought 'em from gun port to gun port. Poured lead right into the middle of the whole group while they sat their horses. Hit at least three of them right off. They retreated, but turned and fired on the house till it shook so, I thought the walls would surely fall down 'round me. Guess they got tired of shootin' after a spell."

"How'd the door get open?"

"Let the dog out to check around 'bout two hours after that bunch rode off. Figured Wolf'd flush out any of them boys as might be hidin' outside to trick me or such. Left the door cracked open so's he could get back in. Then, I dragged Donald over to the fireplace."

A look of total surprise flitted across Longarm's face. "You mean he still lived after being shot flush in the head like that?"

"Oh, no, Marshal. 'Course not. He was already dead as my great-grandpa. Didn't have no more pulse'n a pitchfork. Sat down on the floor with his head in my lap. Got his pistol out'n the holster and laid it on the floor beside me. 'Bout then I heard the ruckus outside. Growlin', barkin', shoutin', shootin', and such-like. From the sound of the fight, I figured Wolf'd done been brought down, too."

"How many stayed behind, Miriam? Do you know?" Kate asked.

"Only seen the one. He come to the door after fightin' off my dog. Come slinkin' up to the door. I played dead till he got inside. Rotten skunk was one surprised outlaw, when I sat up and plugged him twice. Worthless son of a bitch stumbled away. Not sure where he went. Didn't hear no horse gallop off, that's for sure. Figure he's a layin' dead out there under a bush sommers. Leastways I surely hope so. Hope I kilt him deader'n last year's outhouse trench."

Nightshade slid toward the door and said, "I'll take a look around. See if'n I can find him."

Kate reached across the table and took both of Miriam Westbrook's hands in hers. "We're after the men who killed your Donald. The same gang murdered my daughter. So, you see, we can't tarry long. But we'll do anything we can to help. What can we do for you? Just name it."

The Westbrook woman's head swiveled around on her thin neck. She stared at the body of her dead husband for several seconds. Longarm felt sure she would descend into

129

a fit of weeping, but that near certainty never occurred. As if suddenly imbued with a surge of fresh spirit, she stood, then said, "You can help me lift Donald's body up on this table so I can prepare him for the grave. I'll not have him go to God lookin' such a mess."

Chapter 13

Several hours later, Longarm snapped awake. He'd watched Kate help while Miriam Westbrook toiled over her poor, head-shot husband for what seemed nearly an hour. Fatigue finally overtook him, and he'd dropped off to sleep in one of the new widow's ladder-backed kitchen chairs. Standing to stretch the kinks from knotted muscles, he noticed that Orpheus Nightshade lay on the floor in one corner and snored like a hibernating bear.

Their tired arms covered in dried blood, Kate and Mrs. Westbrook moved away from the rough kitchen table and gazed down at their handiwork. Donald Westbrook had been washed, shaved, and dressed in his best Sunday-go-to-meetin' suit. His hair was oiled and combed, eyebrows clipped, and his fingernails cleaned. A look of pleased satisfaction etched Mrs. Westbrook's weary, weathered face when she glanced over at Longarm and said, "Think we've done all we can do for 'im. And now, if you gentlemen would excuse me, I'd like to get myself cleaned up for the buryin'."

Kate yawned, then said, "Me, too. Gonna have to sit on the porch for a spell, boys."

Longarm stumbled over to the rumbling mound that was Orpheus Nightshade and kicked his pontoon-sized foot. The giant sat bolt upright as though he'd been hit by lightning. "Come on, Night. Get up. We gotta vacate the premises and leave the ladies to their twa-let."

Each man carried a cane-bottomed chair onto the covered porch and basked in the reflected, warming glow of the morning sunlight while they each nursed one of Longarm's square-cut cheroots. After several minutes of nothing but sittin' and smokin', Nightshade pointed with his tiny cigar and said, "Family gravesite's yonder on that little hill. Found it last night when I wuz lookin' fer the feller what stuck around after them others rode off."

Longarm stopped chewing his cheroot. "Family gravesite, you say? Do tell. Lady of the house didn't mention anything 'bout a family."

"Yessir. 'Pears they's at least three young'uns buried up there. Maybe more. Kinda hard for me to tell for certain sure, what with it bein' dark and all. But I'm pert sure I did see at least three markers."

"Damned hard life for a woman out here in the wild places with no one but her husband. She told me'n Kate as how she and the dead gent arrived here some thirty years ago."

"Tough row to hoe when you lose yer kids," Nightshade observed, then took another puff from the cigar. "Sure seems to happen a lot these days. Losin' a child's a hard thing to take, but I'd guess it might be even tougher to lose a husband of thirty years."

"I suppose. You know, Night, I musta been asleep when you came back in from your search last night. You find the brigand the lady plugged?"

"Oh, yeah." Nightshade swung his dinner plate of a hand around the opposite direction from the graveyard. "He's laid out colder'n a log-splittin' wedge in Montana.

132

Crawled up under one of them stumpy sage bushes on the side of that little rise over yonder. She popped 'im pretty good. Got 'im twice dead center. Holes couldna been more'n inch apart, right in the notch of his breastbone. Mrs. Westbrook's one helluva shot. 'Peared to me as how once plugged, he set to runnin' from the house, went directly to that very spot, fell to his knees, then crawled up under them bushes and died."

"Find his horse?"

"Yep. If'n the dead feller'd a made it about twenty more yards, he mighta just been able to ride away and die sommers else. But he didn't."

An hour or so later, Longarm and Orpheus Nightshade carried the blanket-wrapped body of Donald Westbrook to a shallow scar in the earth located next to the grave of one of the three children he'd seen die before they lived. Kate Thorne looked on as the solemn men shoveled dirt on the corpse, and watched Miriam Westbrook finally break down.

The rock-solid pioneer woman had carried the family Bible with her for her husband's final trip. Everyone expected her to read a few selected passages to ease his entrance into heaven. But the emotion of the moment destroyed the iron-willed woman's hard-won resolve. She pushed the book at Longarm and, through rivers of tears, said, "Please, sir. Please."

Shocked by the turn of events, and unaccustomed to such graveside performances, Longarm glanced to Kate Thorne for guidance, and even held the book out for her to take. She refused, then said, "Go ahead, Marshal Long. I'm sure whatever you pick to read will be appropriate."

Beads of sweat the size of bullets formed on Longarm's

forehead. From somewhere in a seldom visited portion of his heart and brain the memory of an earlier funeral beside an unmarked grave during the Great War stepped to the front of his thoughts.

After fumbling with the flimsy pages of the Bible for some seconds, the uncomfortable lawman coughed, then said, "Please you, missus, I'll read a few brief passages from chapter fourteen of the Old Testament's Book of Job. *'Man that is born of a woman is of few days, and full of trouble. He cometh forth like a flower, and is cut down: he fleeth also as a shadow, and continueth not. . . . Man dieth, and wasteth away: yea, man giveth up the ghost. . . . Man lieth down, and riseth not: till the heavens be no more.'* And also, from Hosea, chapter thirteen, *'I will ransom them from the power of the grave; I will redeem them from death: O death, I will buy thy plagues; O grave, I will be thy destruction.'* "

As the widow Westbrook took her well-worn Bible back, she sniffled, wiped her nose, then said, "That was perfect, Marshal Long. I could not have asked for better. Not even from a practiced man of the cloth touched with the fire of our maker."

Longarm took the lady's hand in his. An unusual kindness suffused his voice, when he said, "You know, Miriam, I've come to think of death as being kind of like a trip on a ship. It's a journey we'll all eventually have to take. The ticket has already been purchased for each of us. Our reservations are confirmed. And most of us are already more than halfway up the gangplank. One day you'll board the ship as friends and family stand near another spot like this one and say their heartfelt farewells. But when the ship sails and you reach the other side, your husband and all these little ones will be waiting. They'll stand on the shore and call out, 'There. She's coming.' And once again you'll all be together."

The thoughtfulness of his act and the previous night's attendance to the corpse proved too much for Kate Thorne. She dropped to the ground at the widow Westbrook's feet like a sack full of rocks. Longarm lifted her up and carried her to the shade offered near the adobe's covered porch. With Nightshade's help, he placed her in a chair and mopped her brow with a handkerchief made damp with cool water from a bucket the iron-willed Mrs. Westbrook brought from the kitchen.

After a few minutes, the unconscious Kate's eyes popped open. She shook her head as though trying to clear interior cobwebs. "I'm fine," she said. "Swear it. I'm fine." She waved them both aside and stood. "Mr. Nightshade, get the horses. We must be on our way to Raton." She watched her friend hustle away to the corral, then turned to Miriam Westbrook. "Is there anything else we can do before we leave, dear lady? Would you like my companion Mr. Nightshade to accompany you to Trinidad, perhaps?"

Miriam Westbrook clutched the Bible to her breast. "No, there's nothing more you can do for me here, Mrs. Thorne. And, no, I do not wish to go to Trinidad. I'll stay here, for now anyway. This place is where my life has been for the past thirty years, and where the rest of my life remains to be lived."

Nightshade led the trio's animals up, and they all quickly got mounted in a rush of movement and flying dust. Longarm said nothing, but watched and listened as Kate sat her horse and glanced down at the sad woman on the rickety porch. "You're absolutely certain there's nothing more we can do for you, Miriam?"

135

"Oh, I didn't say that, Kate. There is definitely one other small service you can perform for me."

"Name it," Kate said.

"When you find the ghost and his gang, kill 'em. Kill 'em all. And once you've accomplished that glorious task, please take the time to send me word that they're dead so I can go to Mr. Westbrook's grave and tell him that his needless passing has been righteously avenged. Can you do that for me?"

Kate Thorne's face broke into a radiant smile. She glanced from Orpheus Nightshade to Longarm, then back to Miriam Westbrook. "Yes, I can, and I will. You have my word on it."

With those final words, Kate twirled the long-legged black in a tight circle and kicked hard for the road over Raton Pass, as though chased by yellow-toothed demons. Nightshade quickly followed. Longarm took the time to tip his hat, then trailed along behind. Eight miles on the other side of the pass, the town of Raton, filled with miners, gamblers, pimps, fallen women, cattlemen, and killers, waited like a fat black widow spider in a sticky, roughly constructed web.

A steady, ice-flecked drizzle fell late that afternoon when the searchers reined their animals up on a low hill on the southern slope of Raton Pass. In the near dark, Orpheus Nightshade shook his head and muttered, "I made a considered effort not to get close to this hellhole on our way up to Trinidad, Marshal. Didn't want Kate exposed to such a concentrated dose of debauched behavior. Damned place is a snake pit."

Longarm gazed down at the lights. "From what I hear, it is most definitely a hellhole. If not that, it's at least hell's front doorstep. Town's got every form of lowlife scum imaginable workin' the streets. They're as thick as maggots in a rotted corpse."

Kate Thorne put the spurs to her mount and called over her shoulder, "Come on, boys. This jerkwater burg might well be the devil's playground here on earth, but we've got deadly business to conduct there. The man who murdered my daughter is waiting, and I aim to kill him, before he can take anyone else's child."

Chapter 14

As Longarm and his companions urged their animals along the north-to-south expanse of the muddy main thoroughfare of Raton, they entered a once peaceful, territorial village that now suffered from the throes of unfettered good prospects. While beginning to wind down some, feverish work on the nearby Atchison, Topeka and Santa Fe Railway, from Trinidad south to Santa Fe, continued apace.

As a consequence of all the construction, the flow of liquor, gambling, and willing women drew railroaders and line workers of every description—along with hard-rock miners from nearby mountains, enterprising card sharps and gamblers from Fort Worth, scores of trail drovers on their way north to Wyoming or Montana, pickpockets, thieves, soiled doves, flatbackers, hookers, con men, gunfighters, and murderers. Raton teemed with people like an overburdened beehive. Every type of upright, two-legged viper imaginable whooped and hollered from inside rough, false-fronted, disreputable establishments erected on either side of a dirt street that daylight-to-dark traffic had tromped to little more than a muddy quagmire.

Kate guided her straining animal to a hitch rail located in front of a saloon boldly named the Four Deuces and climbed down. An elaborately painted sign over the liquor emporium's covered entrance portrayed a fanned poker hand of the four lowest cards in any deck, along with an ace of spades.

Above the din of racket from the music that flowed into the street, along with that provided by multitudes of shouting people and the occasional popping of gunfire, Kate yelled, "Find a place for all of us to stay the evening, Mr. Nightshade—adjoining rooms, at least one with a bath, if you can arrange it. I am in desperate need of a good scrubbing. Should our efforts here end badly, I am determined not to go before my God smelling like a sweaty pig that just vacated its favorite wallow."

"You bet, Kate. Shouldn't take me too long. Want me to look for somethin' away from all this racket? Maybe a roomin' house outside of town?"

Longarm loosely tied his mount to the hitch rack, lit a cheroot, and watched as Kate Thorne considered Nightshade's suggestion. "No," she said. "Think we need to be as close to the tumult as possible. Don't want anything to go amiss this time. We must be prepared to act in a matter of seconds in order to keep Lomax and his gang of cutthroats from escaping our wrath again."

"Where'll you be, Kate?" Nightshade glanced at Longarm and sneered. "Gonna stay here?"

The spunky woman's face flushed. She turned to Longarm and said, "Could you use a little something by way of liquid refreshment, Marshal Long? I realize that we've had a long, dry day."

Longarm flashed a toothy smile. "Why, yes, ma'am. I surely could."

"In that case, Mr. Nightshade, you can find me and the marshal here inside the Four Deuces once you've finished

140

your search for suitable lodging. It appears that I'm about to buy the marshal a drink."

Nightshade grunted, stomped onto the muck-covered boardwalk, then ambled off through the seething, raucous crowd. The drunken throng moved shoulder to shoulder both ways along the narrow walkway but parted like the waters of the Red Sea to allow his passage.

Longarm touched Kate Thorne's elbow and drew her to a halt just before they pushed through the Four Deuces's bright red batwing doors. "This is very obviously not a place for decent women, Kate. You know that, don't you?"

She tilted her head in the most coquettish manner, threw him a rueful smile, then said, "My dear Custis, since the moment Lomax and his bunch of killers murdered my daughter, then left me barely conscious, lying in the filth of my own barn, I've given very little thought to what 'decent' women do, or don't do. Who knows, keep our wits about us and we might see or hear something inside that could help lead the way to the murdering scum."

"True enough," he said, then pushed the batwings open for her.

Men came nigh to standing on top of one another at the saloon's elaborate polished-mahogany bar. Drunken celebration appeared the order of the evening. Longarm spotted an empty table in the farthest corner of the narrow room. He grabbed Kate by the hand and elbowed his way through the knotty swarm of people. As he reached for a chair to pull it back for the lady, a pair of gamblers in beaver hats, filthy white shirts, silk ties, and pinch-backed coats dove into the seats, slapped brimming glasses of liquor down, then smiled up at him as though they'd won a footrace.

The saddle-weary marshal drew up short, then pulled Kate to a spot behind him. He turned to the grinning idiots at the table and said, "The lady's tired, fellers. She'd like to sit a spell—perhaps have some privacy here in the corner. I trust you gentlemen can find another spot better suited to the conduct of your business."

Kate pulled at his sleeve. "Don't trouble yourself. It's of no real consequence, Custis. It'll be no problem for me to stand until we can find a different seat."

Longarm twisted his head slightly in her direction and hissed back, "It's a problem for me. These dung beetles saw us making our way through the crowd, and they appear to have raced us for the table—a contest I had no idea we were involved in. Now they're darin' me to do something about it."

One of the men snatched his tall hat off and slapped it onto the table, as though to stake a permanent claim. He squinted up at the pair of interlopers, then, in a belligerent and commanding voice, said, "Don't personally give a good goddamn if the *lady* had to crawl all the way over here on all fours like a dog. My friend and I got here first. So, far as I'm concerned the lady can kiss my ass."

With great ceremony, the mouthy gambler's partner fished a deck of cards from his vest pocket, then riffled through them. "We've a game in mind, shit kicker, and would urge you and your *bitch* to get the hell away 'fore it becomes necessary for me to rise up out of this chair and kick your stupid ass till your nose bleeds."

People nearest the action stopped talking. Heads began to turn in their direction. An ugly dispute within minutes of arriving in town wasn't exactly part of Longarm's plan for the evening. But the pock-faced gambler

142

had not only crossed the line, he'd also jumped over it with both feet when he referred to Kate in such a low, profane manner.

At his ear Longarm heard, "I'll take a step back, Custis. You have my permission to handle this situation in whatever manner you see fit. Just please do be careful. They appear quite capable of doing you considerable damage given the right opportunity."

An imperceptible grin flitted across Longarm's lips. He flipped the jacket away from the cross-draw pistol resting on his left side. "Have a suggestion for you card-bendin' bastards. Why don't you apologize to the *lady*, then get off your ample asses and head for the door, before I find it necessary to chastise the both of you."

The hatless man grabbed up the deck of cards from the table and glared at Longarm, as though about to strike out like a cornered rattler. He expelled a huffing sigh of disgust, then leaned back in his chair and tapped a finger against a stubble-covered chin. He flicked the finger at Longarm, and said, "Final warnin', shit kicker. Trundle yourself and *your bitch* on outta here, and we'll forget 'bout the insultin' way you've been actin'."

In a blaze of movement, the mouthy gambler found his nose inside the muzzle of Longarm's Frontier model Colt pistol. Shocked and totally flustered, he slowly raised his hands. Cards fluttered to the floor like snowflakes in a blizzard.

Longarm cut a squinted glance at the second man, then said, "Don't make any sudden moves, boys—either one of you." Over his shoulder he called out, "Kate, would you come over here, please? I think this *gentleman* has something he wants to say to you."

Three-deep into the surrounding multitude, men stopped talking. Whispers buzzed back and forth. The prospect of a killing had grabbed their attention by the throat. A comfortable ring of distance quickly formed around the disputed table.

Kate Thorne strode back up and stopped at Longarm's elbow. Around the barrel of the heavy pistol, the quaking risk taker mumbled, "Sorry, ma'am. Yes, indeed. Truly sorry. Musta lost what little mind I still possess there for a second. Bad whiskey most likely. Makes a man stupider'n a wagonload of rocks. Didn't mean no insult, I assure you. Be most happy to vacate this here chair so's you can sit and take your ease as you see fit."

Longarm came erect again, pulled the muzzle away from the man's nose, and flicked the barrel at the pair in a motion that indicated they could stand. Chair legs made scraping noises on the rough-cut board floor. The duo wobbled to their feet, snatched up their glasses, and hurried away. Jeers, derisive hoots, and laughter from some of those in the crowd closest to the aborted encounter followed them across the room and out the door.

Longarm slipped the Colt back into its holster, then removed his hat and motioned Kate into one of the recently vacated seats. Once the dark-haired beauty was settled, he took a spot at the table that placed his back against the wall. The position guaranteed a view of anyone else who might feel compelled to challenge him.

Kate glanced in the general direction of the gamblers' retreat, then back to Longarm. She placed a comforting hand over one of his. Sounding somewhat distracted, she said, "Do you think they'll be bold enough for a return engagement, Custis?"

He threw his head back and laughed, then said, "Oh, I

doubt it, Kate. I sincerely doubt it. They just headed for the nearest available waterin' hole a bit farther on down the street in search of someone else to intimidate."

A waiter who could have stretched out on the ground under a clothesline during a thunderstorm and not get wet strolled up and made a glancing swipe at wiping the table with a rag that appeared to have once been used to swab the barrel of a cannon. He had the look of someone suffering from intestinal parasites, or worse. "Sorry, folks, the Deuces ain't got no food tonight. Had some sammiches on the bar earlier. This pack of ravenous wolves gobbled 'em all up within ten minutes of me cartin' 'em out from the kitchen."

"Quite all right," Longarm said. "We're not here to eat anyway. You can bring me a glass of Maryland rye, if you have any. Got sarsaparilla for the lady?"

Before the waiter could answer, Kate snapped, "Forget the kid's drink. Bring me a double shot of Kentucky bourbon. Straight. And try to put it in a clean glass."

The waiter's head bobbled. "Why, yes, ma'am. Bourbon in a clean glass. Rye for the gent. Comin' right up. Be right back with your orders, folks."

Longarm watched as the liquor server turned on his run-down heel and vanished into the mass of people milling at the bar. For the briefest of seconds, a look of concern flickered across the lawdog's face when the crowd filled in behind the fleeing man. The unconcerned, smiling appearance that had graced his weathered face a mere second before bled away like spit on a red-hot stove lid.

Kate tried her best to see what might have changed his mood so quickly, but had no luck identifying the culprit. "What is it?" she asked, after several seconds passed and he continued to stare into the swarming mass of people.

As though to himself, Longarm mumbled, "When the waiter pushed his way up to the bar, could've swore I saw Pinky Daggett. Just for a second, mind you, but it sure looked like him."

Kate stared into eyes fixed on the crowd. "Who on earth is Pinky Daggett, Custis?"

Still distracted, Longarm said, "Used to be one of Lomax's chosen. Damned near as heartless as ole Spook, if any of the rumors prove true. He's been widely known to travel with the Lomax bunch in the past. Stretches all credulity that he'd be here in Raton alone, since Lomax is probably somewhere nearby."

The rail-thin waiter elbowed his way out of the crowd once again and bustled back over. He placed the ordered drinks on the table and waited. "That'll be a dollar, mister."

Longarm appeared to react as though someone had slapped his face. "A dollar? Sweet jumpin' Jesus, you bring me twenty cents worth of liquor and want a dollar for it?"

The waiter's bony shoulders levitated upward, then fell in an unconcerned shrug. "That's what the folks who own the Deuces charge. In this town, a body cain't get a drink of anything a human bein' can swaller for less—leastways not since all these railroaders showed up, near a year ago."

Longarm held a five-dollar gold piece over the palm of the man's skeletal hand. "You can keep it all, if you'll answer one question for me."

A snaggle-toothed smile spread across the waiter's emaciated, hollow-eyed countenance. "Sure thing, mister, if'n I can."

Kate watched as the marshal motioned for the drink slinger to lean closer. She could barely hear it when Longarm said, "First off, tell me your name, son?"

"George. George Crocker."

"Well, George, do you by any chance know a belly-slinkin' snake named Pinky Daggett?"

Crocker snapped a blinking glance back toward the bar. It came and went so quick as to make a person wonder if he'd actually done it, or not. He leaned even closer to his questioner, then said, "Well, for a four-dollar gratuity, I just might know 'im."

Longarm held the gold piece right in front of the man's face. "Do you know him, or not, George?"

Behind his cupped hand, Crocker said, "Hell yes. He's standin' up yonder at the bar, mister. 'Bout midway down. Been rooted to the same spot ever since he came in. You'd think he was a tryin' to keep the bar from tippin' over or somethin'. Him and some others, what looked like they might be cut from the same bolt of cloth, hit the door 'round noon today. Pert sure the rest of 'em left a bit earlier this evenin'."

"What makes you think that?"

"Well, ain't seen any of them others for a spell, that's why."

"How many others, George?"

"Four, maybe five, as I remember."

Longarm dropped the coin into Crocker's palm. He shook his finger in the man's face. "Whatever you do, George, don't mention this conversation to Daggett. Didn't stutter any, did I? You understand my meaning, don't you?"

"Oh, yessir, I understand completely."

Longarm glared at Crocker. "No, George, I'm not sure you do. Revealing our conversation to Daggett before I'm ready for him to be aware of our presence could prove deadly. For the sake of the lady's safety, I'd rather make that fact known at my own convenience. Do you catch my drift now?"

Crocker danced from foot to foot. "Yeah, ain't no doubt in my mind exactly what you meant, mister. My momma didn't raise no idiots. Well, 'cept maybe my brother, Eugene. He got mad at some uncooperative nails when we was kids. Went to swingin' wild and hit his very own self in the head with a hammer. He was just nine years old. Boy never was the same after that."

Longarm waved Crocker away, took a long, satisfying sip from his glass, and watched to make sure the nervous waiter didn't make a beeline straight for Pinky Daggett. He turned back to Kate just in time for her to hit him with, "'For the lady's safety'? Did I hear you right, Custis? Would have thought by now you'd be the last person on earth to be worried about my safety."

"Well, Kate, behind all those weapons you're carryin', you do have a soft, feminine appearance and grace about you. I'm right certain our new friend, George, feels like he's doing a great and honorable service for all of American womanhood by protecting the sanctity of your beautiful person from the likes of Pinky Daggett." He smiled, saluted her with his glass, then threw down the rest of the liquid fire it contained.

"You are a silver-tongued devil when you feel the necessity aren't you, Custis?" Then she matched his bold move by throwing the double bourbon back in one slick swallow.

A snorting laugh escaped Longarm's throat that sounded as though it came from smoke-filled lungs. "You're one helluva woman, Kate," he said.

"Well," she said, "you're just before gettin' a lesson in how true that is." She stood and flipped her coat away from the pistol at her waist.

"What are you about, girl?" Longarm snapped.

"Well, Marshal Long, I'm about to stroll over to the bar

and talk with that snake you just mentioned. See if he can't direct me to Spook Lomax."

"Pinky Daggett?"

"That's the one."

Longarm leapt to his feet, then grabbed her by the elbow. "Now, wait just a minute, girl. We just sat down. Thought you wanted to relax a bit."

"No waiting this time, Custis. If Daggett's still in town, then Lomax must be somewhere nearby. If we don't get it out of him right now, we could miss Spook Lomax again. Orpheus and I've been chasing that murderous bastard far beyond way too long. I'd like to put an end to all this and go back home." She slipped her bowie from the folds of her skirt, ran a thumb along the razor-sharp edge, then shoved the blade back into its sheath. "Just wish I hadn't left my saddle gun outside hanging on the horse."

Longarm wagged his head back and forth, then fixed her in a steely-eyed gaze. "As you wish, Kate, but I'll go first. Let me do all the talkin', and you've got to promise to stay behind me. Agreed?"

"Sure, whatever you say, Custis."

"Don't play with me, girl. Won't have it."

"Said I'd stay behind you, Custis, and I will. Won't get in your way, I promise. Just make sure you get him to tell us exactly what we want to know."

Longarm's fingers tightened on Kate's elbow as he pulled her around behind him. He pushed his coattail back from the belly and hip pistols, then slipped out the gun he carried at his back and held it down by his side, behind his coattail. With Kate in tow, he bulled a path through the drunken throng until they finally reached the bustling tavern's crowded bar.

A pair of dust-covered miners on Longarm's left

slapped empty glasses down on the wooden drink station's polished-marble top, then made quite a ceremony of wiping their mouths on dirty shirtsleeves. Holding each other erect, the inebriated pair stumbled toward the batwing doors and out into the street before Longarm could get his boot propped up on the bar's polished brass foot rail.

As he turned to watch the rock-breakers drunkenly stagger away, Longarm noticed that, standing not six feet down the bar, a bleary-eyed Pinky Daggett had propped himself on his elbows and was nursing a half-filled beer mug of straight whiskey.

Daggett had the hangdog appearance of a down-on-his-luck derelict. The kind of man who'd just lost his last fingernail's hold on anything like a connection to the rest of the world. The kind of man who wanted to kill someone or something, just to get back at all those who'd done him the least kind of wrong in his turbulent past—that was Pinky Daggett.

Longarm could still feel Kate behind him as he took two steps in Daggett's direction, then stopped. He cocked the pistol at his side and waited to see if the drunken outlaw would take notice that hollow-eyed death just might be watching his every move.

Chapter 15

Longarm shot a number of sneaky glances around and behind Daggett. He could detect no other obvious threat. None of the other men standing near the unsuspecting outlaw proved recognizable as a possible menace. Daggett appeared beyond caring if anyone might bother to challenge him, so Longarm said, "Evenin', Pinky."

Daggett's name came out sounding as though the lawman had hocked up a cocklebur and spit it into the man's drink. The outlaw's head swiveled around on his neck like a wooden wheel on an ungreased axle. "Who the fuck are you? I know you? Hell's fuckin' bells, I don't know you." He turned, staggered, slowly brought himself erect, then took another nibbling sip from his mug. He wiped his cracked lips on a filthy canvas coat sleeve. "Naw, ain't no way I ever knew a candy-assed lookin' gob of bar squeezin' like you, mister. Why don't you get the fuck away from me 'fore I grab your ignert-lookin' ass up and bust you out like a festered pimple?" Daggett threw his head back, staggered again, then went into an odd twitching fit like an inmate from an insane asylum. He grabbed the bar to right himself and even attempted to laugh at what he obviously perceived as the funny he'd just pulled.

Longarm smiled—almost laughed—at the man's inability to control his own bodily movements. "Been a long time, Pinky, but you do know me, you scurrilous bastard. Take a good, long look. Think about it for a second, maybe even two or three. Let that liquor-saturated brain of yours do a little work for a change. Arrested you down close to Fort Davis a few years back for attempted robbery of an El Paso bank. Trampled a child during your attempt to escape."

Daggett's eyes narrowed as he tried to get his whiskey-drenched mind around exactly what was happening. His concentration appeared to deepen as he stared over the mug while taking another sip of the potent liquor. All of a sudden, he pulled the beaker away from a mouthful of rotted teeth and pointed with it. "Deputy Marshal Long, ain't it? Custis By God Long. Some even calls you the Longarm of the fuckin' law, or some such silly-assed shit. Hail from up around Denver and other more civilized places north of this horse-shit-smellin' hellhole."

Longarm's grin was genuine the second time. "Now you're gettin' the picture, Pinky. Right flattered a man in your condition has enough unpickled brain left to remember."

Daggett waved at his antagonist with the beer mug. "Well, I ain't got no truck with the likes of you, lawdog. You ain't got no paper on me. This here's New Mexico Territory, not Denver. What the hell you want?"

"Don't bet on me not having any paper on you, Pinky. Besides, I'm a deputy U.S. marshal. We could be standing in Moose Jaw, Alaska, right now having this conversation and I'd still be able to arrest you if I wanted to. Now, how 'bout we step outside to a nice quiet spot where we can actually hear each other talk. Got some questions I want to ask you."

Daggett eased the mug onto the bar, slid it to a spot out of the way of perceived harm, turned, and hooked his thumbs over his pistol belt. "Well, that's what I'd call a thinkin' out'n yer ass, badge toter. Ain't goin' no god-damned where with the likes of you. Got somethin' you want to say to me, you can say 'er right fuckin' here."

Longarm bored in on the drunken skunk. He spat, "I do sincerely believe you should think it over, Pinky. Step on outside with me."

"Tell you what, Mr. Longarm of the fuckin' law, why doan chu just go right on ahead and think in one hand and shit in the other'n. See, by God, which 'un fills up fastest. Better yet, why doan chu write that suggestion on a piece o' paper, fold it five ways, and stick it up yer dumb, badge-wearin' ass."

In his ear, Longarm heard Kate whisper, "I recognize this man, Custis. Either you get him outside this very minute, or I just might be forced to kill him right where he stands."

Before Daggett could even begin stringing an additional pair of coherent thoughts together, Longarm brought his pistol up in a gleam of blued-steel and tapped the drunken outlaw between the eyes with the barrel. He caught the unconscious drunk under the arms as the man's knees buckled and he crumpled toward the floor.

"Grab his other arm, Kate," Longarm said.

On their way to dragging Daggett outside, they literally ran into Orpheus Nightshade on the muddy boardwalk. No explanation of the situation was necessary for the giant. He reached between his friends and grabbed Daggett up by the scruff of the neck like a rag doll. With Longarm and Kate in tow, he dragged Daggett along the boardwalk, then down an alley between the Four Deuces and a busy Chinese laundry.

Hidden behind a stack of empty wooden shipping crates

and broken freight skiffs, away from the prying eyes of all the yahoos passing on the street, Nightshade propped his load atop a convenient, empty whiskey barrel. He stripped the groggy outlaw of all the weapons he could find, then began shaking and slapping the man in an effort to revive him.

Longarm and Kate stood slightly behind and on either side of Nightshade, as Daggett swam back to fuzzy-headed consciousness. The woozy outlaw tried to fend off the frying pan–sized hands smacking his reddened cheeks. "Love of Christ," Daggett yelped, "stop slappin' on me, you son of a bitch."

Gunmetal-colored clouds directly overhead parted long enough for a shaft of brilliant moonlight to fall into the alleyway and illuminate the developing scene. Daggett's rubber-eyed, wandering gaze managed to focus on the monster that had him by the neck. "Sweet leapin' Jesus! You're one big ugly bastard, ain't cha? Your mama a jugheaded horse by any chance?"

Kate Thorne's close friend flashed a teeth-gritting smile, then smacked the outlaw again—harder. Daggett's teeth rattled and his head bounced off the wall of the Chinese laundry like a kid's rubber ball. "Where's Spook Lomax, mister?" Nightshade growled. "Don't be shy, speak right up 'fore I make such a mess outta your mouth it stops workin' altogether. Best be comin' across with somethin' in the way of information pretty quick, or you won't be eatin' much of anything but oatmeal mush for a spell."

For the first time, a look of genuine concern flashed over Daggett's palm-reddened face. He briefly glanced at each of his tormentors, then the fleeting moonlight faded and the alley once again fell into shadowy darkness. "Look, I doan know who'n the bleedin' hell you people are," he grumped. "Don't know any of you from a bag of

154

rock salt, 'cept this here lawman. But, even if I knew all three of ya like brothers and sisters, I ain't tellin' nobody nothin' 'bout ole Spook."

"You should have taken a more thorough look while the moon was out," Kate snarled. She pushed her way around Orpheus Nightshade and got as close to Daggett as she could. "Think you might remember me, if you'd just give my face a bit more thoughtful consideration."

Daggett leaned as close to the angry woman as he could without touching her. His head tilted to one side like a bluetick hound examining a cotton-patch rabbit for the first time. Suddenly he jerked away as though he'd gotten too close to something red-hot, or had his face slapped again.

"Recognize me now, don't you, you murderin' son of a bitch?" Kate purred.

"God Almighty, ma'am. Thought for sure you wuz dead."

Longarm stepped around to Nightshade's free side. "Well, she's not, you stupid gob of spit," he snapped. "Now, Mr. Nightshade here is the lady's dear, dear friend, and he has a pretty short fuse. Seems you were in the company of men who abused this woman, did the same for her young daughter, then killed the child. Best advice you're gonna get tonight is to answer his questions or suffer in ways you can't even begin to imagine. Hell, I can't even begin to imagine them."

Daggett stared at Longarm's shadowy face in the dim light. "Have to do his best, then, Longarm. 'Cause I ain't sayin' nothin' to nobody, about nothin'."

The gleaming blade of a thirteen-inch-long, horn-handled, Arkansas toothpick sparkled in the stingy glow from the moon. Nightshade slapped one enormous hand over the outlaw's mouth, raised the knife-filled paw above

155

the entire party's heads, then plunged downward in a blur. The outlaw let out a muffled squeal that sounded like a stomped-on cat. The dagger passed into his upper thigh, ricocheted off the large bone in his left leg, then pinned the man's stringy-muscled limb to the barrel top.

Nightshade's raspy whisper hissed from between gritted teeth like escaping steam from an Atchison, Topeka and Santa Fe Baldwin engine. "Where the hell is he? Tell me now and save yourself a lot of pain, you mealymouthed weasel."

Weeping from the blistering sting of massive damage done to his leg, Daggett appeared to have suddenly sobered up. Between Nightshade's fingers, he blubbered, "He ain't here, damn you to hell. Ain't in town now, you big son of a bitch. Swear it 'fore crucified, bleedin' Jesus. I'm tellin' you the God's truth."

Longarm reached between Nightshade's thick-as-railroad-cross-ties forearms and pushed the brigand's head up so he could hear him better. "If Lomax isn't here, then where is he? You know, so you'd best spit it out."

"I ain't sure. Honest to God, Marshal, I ain't for ab-solute sure," Daggett boo-hooed.

Nightshade snatched the big knife upward, and out of the outlaw's leg. A sound, totally unfamiliar to the ears of decent people, shot from Daggett's lips and darted toward heaven. A screeching prayer for mercy no one heard, except the three other people in the alley. His head dropped to one side, as though he'd passed out again.

Nightshade ran the backside of the long, thin blade along Daggett's jaw. "You ain't pullin' that on me, you slimy snake. Perk up and pay attention, or I'll pin you to the wall with this here big sticker front to back and leave you hangin' like a gob of rotten fruit."

Daggett brought his head up like a man so tired he could barely move. "Please, God, folks," he sobbed. "Spook, and the only three of his men left alive, as I know of, headed down south to Cimarron earlier this afternoon. Far as I can say, that's where they is right this minute."

"Why?" Longarm growled.

"What?"

"Why'd Spook and the other boys go to Cimarron?"

His head shook like he didn't want to answer, but, finally, Daggett said, "Well, they's some whores down that-a-way Spook favors, you know. Twins. Good-lookin' gals. Redheads, from what I hear. Accordin' to Spook, the crew's supposed to be back sometime early tomorrer, 'fore noon. They 'uz gonna stop, pick me up out front of the Deuces, and then we 'uz all a headin' back to Black Mesa, where it's safe from the likes of you bastards. And that's it. All I know. Ain't sayin' nothin' else 'bout it, by God."

Kate pulled on Longarm's sleeve and led him to a spot a few feet up the alley toward the street. "What do you think about all this, Custis? Should we sit here and wait for the lowlife bastards to come back, or should we go after them?"

Longarm snatched his hat off and ran his fingers through sweaty hair. He stuffed the hat back on, then said, "Personally, I don't see any point in makin' a twenty-five-mile, hell-bent-for-leather ride in the dark, Kate. 'Specially if the whole bunch is comin' back this way tomorrow anyhow. Think it'd be better if we got a good night's sleep, then caught 'em unawares when they come lookin' for ole Pinky. Hell, we can set up shop right out front of the Deuces on the boardwalk early tomorrow mornin'. Should be quite a surprise for ole Spook and his boys, when they ride up."

She glanced at the pair of dim figures farther back in the darkness. "What do we do with Daggett till then? If we turn him loose, you can make bets that he'll warn the others for sure."

"If my most current information is correct, there's no real local law enforcement workin' the streets here in Raton right now. Town has had some law at various times in the past. Mostly work it all through vigilance committees now, though. Town built a jailhouse a few years ago. Has an iron cage inside the building that's big enough to hold four men."

"Where is it?" Kate asked.

"Down on the south end of Main Street, as I remember. We could dump Daggett in there till our business is finished. Throw a piece of chain and a padlock on the door to keep him inside. Or maybe one of us could sit up with him tonight while the other two get some rest."

Orpheus Nightshade hoisted Daggett onto one shoulder like a troublesome sack of flour, then headed for the street. He pushed past Longarm and Kate. "Best find him a sawbones, while you're at it," he said. "This here leg of his is gonna need treatin', or it'll likely fester and start to rot right off in a week or so."

"Well, don't wait for me to be anything resembling sympathetic," Kate snapped. "The murdering sack of rotten manure can fester from his leg to his moustache 'fore I'll help him. And given any chance at all, I'll see to it he doesn't ever have to worry about a bad leg."

Nightshade shifted his load. "You want I should throw his ass down in the street, then hold him whilst you put one in his brain pan, Kate? Hell, I'll do 'er. You know I will. Fact, sounds like a good idea to me."

She shook her head. "Not right now, Night. Suppose it's

probably best we keep the worthless scoundrel alive for a bit longer, old friend. He could very well be lying about everything he's told us so far. If so, we'll want to ask him some more questions tomorrow. Mighty hard to talk to a dead man."

Nightshade chuckled. "Yeah. Really hard to talk to 'em if'n they's dead. And all I need is the word from you and this 'un'll be deader'n a rotten stump, right by God quick."

Longarm retrieved their horses, while Kate and Nightshade stood in the alleyway's shadowy opening and waited. The abandoned jail at the end of Raton's only thoroughfare proved but a short walk to the south. Not a single inquisitive soul who passed them in the hectic street appeared to take the slightest notice of the rough-looking trio. Nor did anyone seem to care that the heavily armed group strode down the middle of the thoroughfare carrying what appeared to be the body of a dead man.

Near the Excelsior Hotel and Bath House, Nightshade pointed and said, "Got three rooms up on the second floor at the back of this place, just like you said, Kate. Had to evict one feller in order to get all of 'em in a row, though. He didn't like it, but didn't really object all that much, once I'd grabbed him by his family jewels, picked him up off the floor, and threatened to rip 'em off."

Dark, musty, and covered in a thick layer of dust, Raton's abandoned marshal's office and jailhouse had obviously not seen any use in months—perhaps longer. Kate rummaged around and scared up a coal-oil lantern with enough fuel left for a bit of flickering, yellow-tinted light. While Longarm watched, Nightshade dumped Daggett's limp body onto an iron-strapped bunk, missing anything like a mattress, inside the lockup's four-man, iron-barred cage.

Daggett groaned and rolled onto his back. Nightshade drew his bowie and expertly sliced off the bottom half of the wounded outlaw's pant leg. He slipped a half-filled pint of whiskey from an inside coat pocket located somewhere beneath the pile of skins that covered him. Without hesitation, he upended the slender bottle over the hole in Daggett's leg, and then shoved it into the open wound. Daggett sat bolt upright, made a strangled, rabbitlike squeak, then promptly passed out. In pretty short order, the fiery liquid began running out the back side of the open wound and dribbling onto the jailhouse floor.

Nightshade waited till most of the liquor had run completely through the wound, then jerked the bottle from the hole in Daggett's leg. He pitched the empty bottle between the bars in the cell window and into the alley outside, then used the ragged chunk of Daggett's rendered pant's leg as a makeshift bandage for the open wound.

When it appeared to Longarm that the man had done about all he could do, Nightshade stood back and admired his medical handiwork in the flickering lantern light. "Seen a surgeon do it like that durin' Mr. Lincoln's War of Yankee Aggression in a hellhole named Pea Ridge. Oughta fix this sorry skunk right up. Whiskey cleaned the wound out 'bout as good as it can be done. Oughta stop the bleedin' and keep any putrefaction from gettin' a toehold as well. Bet the son of a bitch'll be up and dancin' in a couple of days." He scratched his chin, grinned, then added, "That is if'n Kate don't kill him first."

Longarm shook his head, then stepped over to the wobbly office desk near the front door. He slid the contrary top drawer open and spotted a fist-sized iron padlock with the brass key still inside. The rusty device was stiff, but worked. He held the lock up and said, "Well, my friends,

160

bet this is for the hasp on the front of the cage. Guess we won't have to go lookin' for a piece of chain and a lock of our own after all. And since we can pen him up nice and tight, all of us should be able to get a much needed night's rest before tomorrow's dance with Spook Lomax."

Ten minutes later the bone-weary trio stood in the shabby second-floor hallway of the Excelsior Hotel. Nightshade said, "Figure Kate should take the room in the middle in case we need to come to her aid durin' the night. I'll set up camp in the one closest to the street, Marshal. Noise from the street won't bother me none. You can have this 'un." Nightshade disappeared through the door to his room.

Run-down and rung out, Longarm cast a tired nod toward Kate Thorne. "Be best if you leave the adjoining door between your room and mine unlocked, Kate. Wouldn't want to have to shoot my way inside, just in case anything wayward occurs durin' the night."

From the cracked dooway of her room Kate smiled. "How thoughtful of you, Custis. Wouldn't want you to *have* to shoot your way into my bedroom," she said, winked, then closed the door.

Chapter 16

Longarm hadn't waited for Kate to answer or comment. He pushed the door to his room open and immediately dropped into bed. Muscle-wearying fatigue went all the way to the bone. He lay with his eyes closed for a moment and thought to himself that even his hair seemed to ache. Then, after almost dozing off several times, and in spite of the exhaustion, he forced himself to sit up and remove all his firearms and clothing. Nothing worse than waking up in the middle of the night, sweating like a pig, fully dressed, lying on top of a Colt pistol, he thought.

The weapon he normally carried at his back went under the pile of flattened pillows. He placed his hip gun in an easy-to-access spot beneath the bed. And he laid the Frontier model Colt on the rickety nightstand, so it was within easy arm's reach.

Stripped completely naked, he crawled between a set of reasonably clean sheets and gifted himself with a long, luxurious stretch. In a matter of seconds, sleep dropped over the weary lawman like a warm, well-used blanket during a Montana blizzard.

Longarm's dreams that night came on vague and slow, obscured by a warm, pleasant, blue-tinted miasma—a thin, gauzy, curtainlike veil that lightly draped itself over his unconscious mind. The mist rolled and swirled like a distant, formless summertime cloud. It appeared as if someone was moving inside the whirling haze. He fumbled for an explanation while in the throes of deep sleep, but couldn't detect the identity of the person hidden within the vaporous screen.

His unconscious mind groped with the unknowable, and he somehow determined, in his tossing and turning, that the phantom was a woman. Didn't know how he knew, but he knew. Gradually, but with a sense of growing urgency, he swam back through the pleasing, comfortable barrier of deep slumber and snapped to wakeful consciousness—alert, but relaxed at the same time.

When Longarm's eyes blinked open, he awoke lying on his side. Soft, intermittent moonlight bathed the room in a subtle glow that made it easy to see. His gaze quickly landed on the pistol he'd placed on the nightstand. But he soon realized the warmth and voluptuous form of a totally naked woman lying pressed against his back. That insight delayed any thought of serious effort by way of deadly action. Like white-hot coals, erect nipples burned into his flesh. Scorching breath from moist lips caressed his ear. She had reached around his waist. A volcanically heated hand had already massaged his impressive prong into a state of hardness similar to that of the barrel on a Sharps Big .50.

"You won't need the gun, Custis," Kate Thorne breathed into his ear. She gently pulled him onto his back. "Leastways, not the one on the table. Maybe this big popper in my hand, but not the Colt."

In the blurred mental fog created by the combination of axle-dragging fatigue and being awakened from the contentedness of snoring like the righteous, Longarm struggled to say, "What're you doin', girl?" While still a bit muddled-brained, he immediately knew how stupid the question must have sounded. Hell, he could feel what she was doing. He tried to shake the cobwebs out of his head and slapped a palm over his eyes.

Kate raised herself to one elbow, then kissed his cheek—a tender, affectionate, almost chaste peck near the corner of his mouth. "I've not been with a man in a very long time, Custis."

"Got that impression from earlier discussions."

"Not since my husband's passing. Buck was never the same after Orpheus helped him get back home from the war," she said, then licked her way to his belly. "He never fully recovered from wounds sustained at the Battle of Pea Ridge. And he found it impossible to rekindle anything like desire for a wife, not even till the day he eventually died. I hope you'll keep that in mind tonight."

The sadness of the tale, and the boldness of her urgency, surprised and pleased him. Taken aback, but thrilled by the truly unexpected turn of events, Longarm pushed his way up in the bed, then propped himself against a pair of bunched pillows set against the unpainted iron bedstead. He caressed Kate's dark tresses, then tenderly ran dancing fingers down her lean, muscular back. He cupped a beautifully shaped, rounded buttock made powerful by years of ranch work and time spent bouncing in a saddle.

For reasons he couldn't quite put a finger on, a feeling of unaccustomed doubt as to exactly what was about to happen sputtered across Longarm's mind like thousands of tiny, flashing needles. "You've evidently given this entire dance some thought, it seems. But I do feel compelled to ask a very important question, Kate. You are sure about this, aren't you? Absolutely, positively, certain? No doubts? No hesitation?"

A tongue of damp flame flicked its way around the head of his rigid cock. She stopped for a second, continued to stare at the colossal wonderment in her hand, then said, "Given the circumstances, as I understand them, we could both die tomorrow, Custis. Who can know what the future might hold? Especially when considered in the face of bracing a man like Spook Lomax and his henchmen. I've made up my mind. Won't go out of this life saddled with the regrets of what might have been."

"I see."

"And if, please God, we manage to make it through the firestorm, when Lomax finally shows himself, whatever happens tonight could prove a pleasant memory I'll carry with me for the rest of my life. Hope to look back as an old woman on this experience and smile at my wanton and uncommon behavior. Even if I'm gray-haired, toothless, and can't eat anything but soft, mushy food with my fingers."

As tenderly as possible, he pulled Kate's face up and pressed his moistened lips to hers. Her hungry mouth sprang open, and their tongues dueled with each other for dominance. For a tall, robust woman, he discovered that her breasts, while completely adequate, tended toward the small side—perhaps no larger than a man's fist—but the stiff nipple and hardened areola he stroked with an insistent finger and thumb while their openmouthed tongue-sucking continued, were huge.

When she finally broke the lingering kiss and began licking her way back down to his taut rod, he chuckled. Then, to the top of her head, he said, "Your friend, the very impressive Mr. Orpheus Nightshade, ain't gonna come roarin' in here like a wounded grizzly, jerk me outta this bed by my ears, then pitch me through the window into Raton's main thoroughfare, will he?"

Kate halted her carnal efforts at enflaming him to action long enough to say, "Well, not before he pulls those ears to the back of your head and ties them in a bow knot."

"Now, that's comforting. Exactly what I wanted to hear."

"You can relax. He's asleep, Custis. And when Orpheus goes to sleep, you could fire a Napoleon cannon at the foot of his bed, and the noise wouldn't wake him. Man goes to his slumbers like the blameless dead."

The words had barely died on her lips, when she went back to gently massaging the rampant brute between his legs. Then, with a skill that belied her years of absence from the joy obtained by way of bodily pleasures, Kate Thorne expertly tickled the incredibly sensitive spot at the very base of Longarm's balls. Shuddering, his hips rose from the mattress as an eager body silently begged for as much of her concentrated attention as she was willing to provide. Eventually, she again replaced talented fingers with the wide blade of her scorching tongue.

At a point when Longarm felt certain he might not be able to control the culmination of the action, the single-minded girl suddenly rose to her knees. While maintaining her grip on his cock with one hand, she threw a shapely leg over his waist. She guided his stiff-as-a-cavalry-saber love muscle to the portals of the moist, waiting warmth of her inmost being. Then she carefully slid down onto it, until the dripping, blood-engorged labial lips of her sex were pressed tightly against him.

The velvety slickness of her steaming cooch damned near drove him to distraction. For several brain-spinning seconds, Longarm wondered if it was possible for them to be forcibly pulled apart. He grabbed her by the hips and pulled her down even tighter to ensure the seal wasn't broken. Intense waves of heat rippled from the middle of his back. They ran through his balls all the way to the tip of a stony tool that was so hard he felt as though the thing might well crack from end to end.

To his complete surprise, Kate Thorne refrained from descending into a frenzied, howling, bucking fit of bouncing around on his unbending shaft like a good many women he'd known in the past. Instead, the seemingly entranced girl closed her eyes and began a slow, strenuous, grating movement of her superheated crotch against his pubic bone. She moved from side to side at first, then back and forth, as though in an effort to mesh their disparate parts into a single, sex-drenched, molten whole. Then, for several minutes, she somehow managed to twirl her talented pussy in a tight, shaft-sucking circle.

After some minutes, she leaned forward at the waist and welded her flushed, sweating upper body against his. She clamped him in a viselike hug and still managed to continue with the sticky grinding. When he moaned beneath her and levered upward with his hips, she hunched her powerful ass downward against his steaming body and reinforced the sweaty nipple-to-nipple clinch with even more enthusiasm.

"Good Lord Almighty, Kate. Honest to God, girl, feels like you're tryin' to smother me. It's hotter'n San Antonio in July under you right now."

Eyes squinted shut, she appeared sightless and incapable of understanding anything he said, or answering. Her breath came in brief, choppy snorts and gasps. All of a sudden, she snapped back up into a sitting position. The circular rotation of her hips and pussy never ceased. The friction between their legs became ever more heated and intense.

168

From the notch at the top of her hair-covered pubis, to her flame-colored ears, Longarm noted that Kate's body appeared swathed in a deep, pulsing flush. When the aggressive action between them appeared to have achieved its most powerful stage, she threw her head back, swayed from side to side, then let out one long, gasping sigh.

"Hot damn," she yelped. "Oh yes, oh yes. God Almighty, yes! Please. Oh, please. Cut it loose, Custis. Fill me up. Go ahead. Do it. Come on. Come on. Don't hold that big stallion back."

A gushing explosion, which appeared to emanate from the very core of her being, enveloped Longarm's well-lubricated cock with a rippling, squirting massage that felt like it went on for several minutes. Ten seconds into Kate's energetic climax, both hands shot up to her rock-hard breasts and, for several seconds, she amazed him with how violently she pinched and squeezed her own nipples. Jesus, he thought, that's gotta hurt like hell.

Dormant, unused muscles inside her clutched at his retreating rod. The powerful spasms were a futile effort to keep him from withdrawing from her satiated, but still grasping body.

Drenched in sweat, Kate rolled to one side, then onto her back. She propped her head on one arm and groaned, "God, that was wonderful. Just wonderful. Exactly what I needed."

Vaporous steam rose from Longarm's body, as his eyes slowly closed. Within seconds, he snored away like the big blade in a steam-operated sawmill. Beside him lay a still panting Kate Thorne. An hour or so later, still stark naked, the smiling girl slipped from the bed and quietly padded back to her own room. When he awoke the following morning, his memory of the whole experience seemed more like a pleasant, fleeting dream than actual reality.

Chapter 17

Longarm dragged a chair from inside the Four Deuces to a spot near the porch pillar nearest the saloon's entrance. He dropped into the unpadded seat, then flipped the collar of his coat up against the bone-chilling wind that whipped down the street from the north.

He propped a booted foot against the veranda's crudely painted four-by-four support, laid the sawed-off shotgun across his lap, then pulled a cheroot from his coat pocket and lit it. While the icy breezes whipped at his pants' legs, a brilliant sun in a cloudless sky still managed to offer some warmth to the spot he'd picked to wait for Spook Lomax's arrival.

He puffed his smoke to bright, fiery life, then flipped the still burning match into the near deserted street. For about as far as he could see in either direction, Raton appeared to have finally settled down after a full-bore night of rippin' and snortin'. An evening's worth of hell-raising comparable to any he'd witnessed, or even heard about, in Silver City, Durango, or Cheyenne.

Near as Longarm could tell, almost all the action had moved to a number of busy staging areas north of town. Several Texas trail herds and a half dozen wagon trains made up primarily of freight shipments had begun the slow, crowded crawl up Raton Pass, on their way north to Trinidad, Denver, and points north.

. In pretty short order, the now fully awake and sharp-as-a-tack lawman got his nest wallowed out. But he'd barely settled in good when a stinking pile of rags with legs, accompanied by an odor that defied description, staggered up the street and stopped less than ten feet away. A half-empty whiskey bottle dangled from one of the apparition's grime-covered, talonlike hands.

"Thish here got-damned place open fer business, mishter?" the filthy-faced drunk slobbered, then turned his bottle up and took a wicked swig of liquid breakfast.

Longarm blew a smoke ring the size of a washtub in his inquisitor's direction. He hooked a thumb over his shoulder and said, "As I understand it, pardner, this here joint never closes. Last night, heard some passin' waddie say the bartenders inside will most likely be slingin' liquor all day on the day Gabriel blows his golden trumpet to announce the Second Coming."

The wild-eyed derelict waved his jug at Longarm, then took another long, slobbery hit. Most of the fiery liquid appeared to go in one side of the souse's mouth, dribble out the other, then drain its way into a scruffy-looking, ragged, straw- and twig-filled beard.

The besotted man wiped his chin on a filth-encrusted sleeve. "Well, thash damn good ta hear," he said, then picked at the trash in his beard for several seconds. "Had ta sleep in a got-damn livery stable lash night. Think I done picked up some fleas, lice, or some other such bitin' kinda varmints. Chiggers is the worst. Tiny, little sumbitches make me itch somethin' fierce. Hate 'em."

"Life's a hard, mean, hateful bitch ain't it?" Longarm mumbled.

The nameless sot held his free hand up and said, "Thish here look lack a spider bite to you? Been itchin' me like a sumbitch. An' worse, by a damn sight, 'pears like I might be a startin' ta run low on giggle juice. Thish 'un here's my lash bottle. Gonna haf'ta stock up some, I 'spect. Done got so's I cain't make it through a whole day 'thout a gallon, or so, of bonded in the barn scamper juice."

Longarm nodded, as though on the verge of being bored slap out of his skull, then reached inside his jacket and pulled out his wallet. He removed the deputy U.S. marshal's star that he usually carried there, then pinned it on the front of his coat. When finished, he glanced up again and noticed that the future gut-puking, knee walker had intently watched his every move. The foul-smelling slug, who couldn't have hit the ground with his hat, acted as though this particular show was the most entertaining thing he'd seen in years.

Swaying like a weeping willow in a cyclone, the inebriate took another long, loud, sucking gulp from his dwindling supply of gator sweat. He corked the bottle, then, sounding belligerent, said, "Yew a got-damned lawman, mister? Star toter? Got-damned lawdog? Got Almighty, but I do hate a got-damned lawman. You sumbitches been the bane of my existence since I wuz seven years old. 'Member as how Marshal Harvey Trotter arrested me on my seventh birthday fer settin' a Baptist church house on fire back in Miz-uri. Put my little ass in jail, too. Said them hardshell believers didn't take lightly to havin' the house of the Lord torched by the likes of me."

"I'm a deputy U.S. marshal out of Denver, old-timer."

"Old-timer? Did I just hear yew call me old-timer? Got a lotta got-damn nerve callin' me old, mister deputy U.S. marshal outta Denver. As a matter of pure-dee fact, yew can jus' bend over'n fuck yerself. Fuck yew an' yer got-damn horse, too, by Got. Where is your horse, by the way, lawman? I'll just go ahead on and lay the hammer to 'im right now whilst I'm thinkin' 'bout it."

Longarm shook his head in disgust, then glanced almost directly across the street and spotted Orpheus Nightshade propped against the door frame of an abandoned leather-working shop. Nightshade tapped the brim of his floppy felt hat with one finger and nodded. "No need to go and get your eyes all walled up and your neck bowed, old-timer," Longarm said.

"Gubberment lawman, huh? Worst kinda got-damn law pushers they is. Worse'n any 'em local boys. Ain't got no use fer none of yuz. But you gubberment types is the ab-salewt fuckin' worst." The drunk's face reddened to the point where his head looked as though it might explode.

Longarm's patience had begun to wear mighty thin. Of all the times this yahoo could have picked, he thought, he sure as hell didn't need this kind of aggravation today. "Calm down, mister. Gonna have a stroke if you don't."

The heap of rags stumbled up a pair of rickety, difficult-to-negotiate wooden steps, then wobbled his way onto the boardwalk. He waved the bottle like a club. Rheumy eyes swam in his head like cherries in a snow bank. His frac-tured mind appeared to bobble around for a spell, then he finally managed to settle on a previous thought that dealt with the question of his age. "Yew're one hard to convince sumbitch, ain't 'cha? Never met a law bringer what wasn't. Ain't but tweny-seben year old, you gubberment, star-totin' sumbitch. My lash birfday. Tweny-seben. Ain't no got-damned old-timer."

No longer than the discussion had lasted, Longarm was already tired of the pointless exchange. "Just nothing worse than trying to talk with a man whose brain's been eaten up by whiskey," he grumbled to himself. Might as well try to reason with a water trough full of horse piss, he thought.

He pointedly ignored the intoxicated annoyance for a second, then cut another quick glance across the street. His gaze landed on a figure seated a few doors to the south of Nightshade's chosen spot. Kate Thorne had adopted the part of a local lady who'd relaxed for a second on a bench in front of a ladies millinery shop—a near perfect ruse for the day's deadly business. The saddle rifle she'd used like an ax on Henry Hatchett's rock-hard noggin was discreetly propped by her side.

Quick as a cat, Kate took notice of Longarm's gaze, and, ever so slightly, she smiled and nodded in response. He'd tried to dissuade her from attendance at the coming dance during breakfast that morning. His arguments fell on deaf ears that still glowed with the previous evening's carnal fun and games. No doubt about it, in Longarm's mind, the girl was fired up.

"I've come this far," she said. "You'll not keep me from the satisfaction of being there when Lomax and his bunch are brought down. So don't even bother to bring the subject up again. Just stop yammering and let's get on with the killing."

Without looking at the irritating, foul-smelling wad of bar squeezings not five feet away, and, as if to himself, Longarm muttered, "Best get off the street, friend. Gonna be some deadly action out here shortly. Wouldn't want any harm to come your way. Be a shame for a man who's devoted so much time and effort to killin' himself with liquor to end up dyin' of lead poisoning."

The snort and snoozer straightened up as though a gold-braided, brass-bottomed Union cavalry colonel had just stepped up and called him to attention. He did a smartly executed about-face toward the street and gave the entire length of the thoroughfare a wide-eyed, lingering examination.

"What the hell 'er yew talkin' 'bout?" he grumped. "Damned street's almos' empty. Ain't hardly no one even up and around yet. Looks like St. Jo, Miz-uri on any Sunday mornin' you'd wanna pick. Swing a cat and yew ain't gonna hit a livin' fuckin' cizzzen, soul, or person. 'Cept maybe that gret big sumbitch over yonder 'crost the street. Good Got, he's a one monster, ugly cocksucker."

Movement at the south end of Raton's central thoroughfare brought Longarm to his feet. He thumbed the hammers back on both barrels of the shotgun and laid it in the crook of his left arm. From the corner of his eye, he saw both Nightshade and Kate quickly follow suit. Then, without so much as a glance at the man, he said, "Do yourself a big favor, mister. Get the hell off the street. Do it now. Don't wait."

Ignoring Longarm's pointed instructions, the ragged drunkard followed the lawman's gaze just in time to spot four riders as they emerged from a swirling curtain of dust. The roiling cloud appeared to have come out of nowhere. It hung in the air as though nailed to the sky like the dried skins of dead animals.

"Jesus," the pile of rags grunted. "'At 'ere's Spook Lomax an' some of his gang, lawdog. Fuckin' bad bunch. Year 'er so ago, I personal seen 'im beat a feller slap to death down in Buckeye. Used a pair of red-hot horseshoe tongs. Snatched 'em right off'n a blacksmith's fire. Beat on 'at poor bastard till wasn't nothin' lef' but a greasy spot in the public roadway. Made one helluva mess."

Longarm switched the shotgun to his right hand and

held it down against his leg. He swept the drunk aside with his free arm and pushed the uncooperative, staggering man toward the Four Deuces's batwing doors. "Get inside, you stupid son of a bitch—unless you're hellbent on dyin' a bloody death this very day."

With the area around him safely cleared of anyone who might get hurt by errant gunfire, Longarm pulled his hat down over his eyes, leaned against the porch pillar like a common street loafer, and continued to puff on the cheroot. Beneath his hat brim, he knifed a glance across the street and noted that Kate and Orpheus were making every effort to appear equally inconspicuous.

Kate had turned her back and gazed into the millinery's window, as though simply shopping for a new hat or dress. But Longarm could tell her attention was totally centered on the ethereal, reflected images approaching in the shop's glass window. Nightshade had moved into the street and taken a spot behind a horse tied at a convenient hitch rail. Longarm could see the hand-carved leg amidst those of the horse. Good move, he thought, damned animal is probably the only thing in the street big enough to actually hide most of him.

Longarm turned his complete attention to the quartet of gunmen. They oozed out of the odd, churning cloud and slowly moseyed up the street. All four wore grayish white, knee-length dusters over their other clothing and rode with wide-brimmed hats pulled low over slitted eyes. Every third step the horses took, Lomax tilted up his pale, ghostly face and perused the boardwalks on either side of the street.

Two doors down from the Four Deuces, the entire party reined to an abrupt halt. All four men appeared to dismiss any other possible threat on the street and concentrated considerable interest onto Longarm's lone figure.

Lomax stepped down from a long-legged gray—a beast that contributed mightily to the spectral image he appeared to carefully cultivate. The duster swirled around him as his leg came over the animal's rump. Jesus, Longarm thought, he does, for a fact, look exactly like every kid's most common image of a phantom seen only in nightmares.

Like a trio of machines, Lomax's henchmen followed their leader. The group drifted along behind him as the Ghost of Black Mesa led them to a hitch rail on the Four Deuces's side of the street.

Animals safely tied, the Spook made several silent hand gestures. The sullen party of killers formed into a ragged line—each man about arm's length from the next—that spread halfway across the street. Almost simultaneously, all of the villains flipped their dusters away and exposed an arsenal of weapons that bristled from bullet-studded gun belts. In a matter of seconds, the Lomax gang ambled up to Longarm and came to a jingling standstill in the middle of Raton's empty, windblown street.

The company of killers stood not five steps from Longarm's chosen spot on the Four Dueces's piece of board-walk. They glared up at him like red-eyed demons from hell. One of them spotted the deputy U.S. marshal's star on Longarm's chest. As if by some sort of unspoken black magic, that bit of information sped from one end of the line of gunnies to the other.

Longarm's head came up. At the same time he leveled the shotgun directly at the Ghost of Black Mesa's hollow, sunken chest. "Been waitin' for you, Spook."

Weird, dead eyes, a shade of pink near that of bubbling, chest-wound blood, gazed back at Longarm. "I know you." The voice sounded like it belonged to a man who'd had his throat cut with a piece of rusted barbed wire. "Custis Long.

Deputy U.S. Marshal Custis Long. Interrupted some of my fun a few years back, as I recall. Even tried your best to kill me. Came mighty nigh on to doin' it, too, if'n memory still serves. Shot me twice."

Longarm ignored the three other men. He'd worked it out with Nightshade and Kate at breakfast. They would see to the disposal of any Lomax henchmen who showed up, if necessary. He wanted the Ghost to himself, and he wanted the man dead so bad his liver itched. A quick glance revealed that Nightshade already had his rifle leveled at the group, and Kate brought the saddle gun up at the ready. The trap was set, now all Longarm had to do was spring it.

A mouthful of rotted teeth showed when Lomax grinned and grunted, "You come to arrest me, Long? Lotta good men've tried to put me in chains in the past. They're all pushin' up daisies now."

"No doubt about it, you're a real bad man."

"Damned right, Long. I've looted, raped, and pillaged. Murdered men, women, and children all over Wyoming, Colorado, New Mexico, and Oklahoma Territory. Done my share of killin' in Texas, as well. Last I bothered to count I've kilt nigh on sixty people. Could be I've even kilt some I can't remember anymore. Wouldn't surprise me a bit. Think you might find the task of arrestin' a man as bad as me some difficult to pull off, bein' as how they's four of us and only one of you."

Longarm flashed a broad, toothy grin. "Well, you don't have to worry yourself none 'bout bein' arrested, Spook. Go on ahead and talk as bold as you like."

"Oh, I will, and fuck you very much, Long."

"Didn't come to make no arrests today, you ugly, skulkin' son of a bitch. Don't even carry anything like official paper on you—no wants, no warrants, nothin'."

179

Lomax swayed, as though unable to fathom the mystery. "Then why're you here, lawdog?"

"Well, it's like this, Spook. You've been declared expendable, superfluous. No longer necessary—if a rabid weasel like you ever was. You're a walkin' dead man, and just too stupid to know it."

Lomax flinched, then took half a step backward. If it were possible to become paler than pale, he managed the trick. An uneasy buzz whipped through his crew of villainous followers. "What the hell does that mean? Su-per-fluous. Fuckin' ten-dollar word, if'n I ever heard one. Didn't have any idea you badge-totin' bastards was smart 'nuff for ten-dollar words like su-per-fluous."

The trace of a wicked smile creaked across Longarm's lips. "Means your presence among the living is no longer required, you ignorant wretch. You're unneeded. Your time on this earth is up. Over. The sand has definitely run out of your hourglass. *Finis.* Satan is personally waitin' for your lily-white, ugly-assed appearance on his front doorstep. And I've come to the asshole of the West to put an end to your horrors and send you on your way to that horn-tailed demon of the pit."

The series of tiny, unrelated events that followed were so slight anyone uninitiated in exactly what the face of death looked like would probably not have noticed them. Longarm spotted many, if not all of them. Here, an almost imperceptible spasm at the corner of Lomax's puckered, fishy-looking mouth. There, a twitching finger that tapped the walnut butt of the big Remington pistol boldly lying across his stomach. And men around Lomax who toed the anxious line of the imminent dead and got that wild-eyed look of anxious, uncontrollable action about to explode from within.

180

Longarm tightened his finger on the shotgun's trigger. But before he could squeeze off a barrel of heavy-gauge, wad-cutter buckshot, there was a thunderous explosion and Lomax's hat flew off. The front-to-back shot exited just over the Ghost's nose, whistled past Longarm's ear, and lodged in the door frame behind him.

The dreaded murderer's head exploded in a shower of white hair, brain matter, blood, and bone that rocked Lomax onto his toes, then dropped him to the manure-covered street like an empty shuck. So effective was the whistling slug's placement, the most feared man in the West didn't even twitch once he'd landed face-first in the dirt and muck.

Longarm swore, then cast an astonished, fleeting glance toward the boardwalk directly behind the group of outlaws as all three remaining gunmen whirled to confront the death-dealing threat. Smoke still rose from the barrel of the Winchester saddle rifle clutched in Kate Thorne's hands. She jacked another shell from the magazine loading tube into the breech, but something inside the weapon went horribly wrong. The shell jammed, and Longarm watched as she fought to get the hung lever back up. Orpheus Night-shade roared like a wounded grizzly and stepped into the street to divert attention his way.

All three of Lomax's remaining gang members filled their hands with pistols. "Don't do it, boys," Longarm yelled, then dropped to his stomach on the porch and rolled to a spot behind the four-by-four porch support.

Thunderous, general gunfire aimed in three different directions at the same time broke out from every man in the street who could still stand and hold a weapon. A near deafening, cannonlike racket from all the discharged pistols ricocheted off the surrounding buildings and raced up and down the nigh empty street like a herd of stampeding cattle.

A stream of 250-grain slugs ripped into the Four Deuces's front wall, notched the planks around the spot where Longarm fell, and bored holes in the narrow shaft of safety afforded by the porch pillar. Horses reared and squealed in terror at the hitching posts on both sides of the street. One unfortunate beast went down in a heap of squealing, blood-slinging flesh. Poor animal tried to get up, then ran in place till its heart gave out.

As if caught in a bad dream, slowed by air somehow saturated with molasses, Longarm watched as the desperate gunny nearest Kate did a spectacular, dancelike spin in the dirt. He saw Kate glance up in confused terror as though unable to fathom the unfolding events she'd personally set in motion. The killer dropped to one knee and ripped off at least four shots with deadly accuracy before Orpheus Nightshade managed to splatter the villain all over most of the street and both of his friends.

Longarm gritted his teeth. He knew it was too little, too late. Kate Thorne went down in a heap in front of the millinery's sheet of polished plate glass. The window shattered in a storm of sparkling pieces and rained down on top of her motionless body like millions of tiny, jagged icicles.

An involuntary scream, executable only by Rebel fighting men who survived Mr. Lincoln's War of Yankee Aggression, escaped Longarm's pained chest. He dropped the hammers on both both barrels of the .10-gauge Greener at the same time and swept the street clean of the two remaining players. Both men went down in bloody heaps before they could find it within their stupid, unrepentant selves to do any serious damage.

A blanket of burnt black-powder smoke still hung in the air when Longarm and Orpheus Nightshade both knelt on the boardwalk beside the bullet-riddled body of Kate Thorne. In the instant when Nightshade turned her over both men knew beyond any doubt that she was no longer with them. Even so, a beatific aspect of peace and a slight smile graced her handsome face.

Longarm could do nothing but turn away from the scene, lay his shotgun aside, tiredly remove his hat, then place a head that throbbed like cannons on a battlefield in his hands. From between his fingers he watched as Kate's gigantic companion held the lifeless girl in his arms like a broken doll. The bearlike man threw his head back and howled like the only wolf left alive in the big cold and lonely. Pimply chills brought on by Nightshade's unearthly cries ran up and down Longarm's back like a carpet of icy chicken flesh. He couldn't recall ever hearing such a pain-filled voice before—except during the worst parts of the Great War.

U.S. Marshal Billy Vail leaned back in his chair and let out a long, sad sigh. He'd listened with keen interest as his favorite deputy related the entire sad tale of how Spook Lomax had finally been brought to book. Now, he felt tired to the bone himself and deeply saddened by the obvious pain he saw etched on his friend's face.

"You accompanied the lady's body back to her ranch?"

Longarm squirmed deeper into the morocco leather chair. He glanced up at the ceiling of Vail's office, took a puff from his cheroot, then stared at his hand as though he'd never seen it before. "Yeah, Billy. Beautiful spot down in New Mexico Territory. Out in the Cornudo Hills, where the Mora River meets the Canadian. Me'n Nightshade buried her on a little tree-shaded hill not far from the ranch house in a spot between her husband and daughter. Said me and Nightshade, but, I must admit, he dug the hole. Tried my best to help him, but he wouldn't let me. Said he'd buried the other two and felt compelled to see that Kate got put to rest himself."

"Well, I never thought anyone else except Lomax would end up dead when I sent you out after him."

Longarm stood, stuffed his hat on, then pulled at the brim. "I understand that, Billy. Best-laid plans and all that kinda stuff. Hell, you just can't ever know what's gonna transpire when you're dealin' with bad people. Can't predict who'll die and who won't when guns come out and people start killin' one another."

"What about Nightshade? Think he'll make it all right?"

"He's somethin', no doubt about it. You know, after the burial, he told me as how, after the Battle of Pea Ridge, he'd carried Buck Thorne on his back all the way from Arkansas to that little ranch on the Mora. Had to walk the whole way on a leg that had a mini ball in it. Leg finally went bad, but he kept on a goin'. Local sawbones had to take the rotten, festered thing off once he finally delivered his friend back home. Personally, can't imagine how he managed to stay alive. Perhaps even more difficult, I can't fathom that kind of friendship."

"Amazing."

"Yep. Quite a story, Billy. I've often wondered what it must be like to have friends like that."

"What about Pinky Daggett?"

"Turned him out 'fore me and Nightshade left for Kate's ranch. Didn't have any reason to bring him in.

Miracle of miracles his leg was already better. Guess Orpheus knew what he was doing with that whiskey bottle. Well, I'm tired, Billy, think I'll head home and get some rest."

Vail followed his deputy to the door of the office. He placed a comforting hand on Longarm's shoulder. "Look, Custis, there's not much goin' on right now. You take some time off. I'll send for you, if anything important comes up. Get some rest. Get your mind right."

"Actual time off, huh? Must be gettin' a bit senile in your old age, Billy." He stopped and turned to his friend. "Really liked that gal, you know, Billy. Don't run across too many like Kate Thorne out in the wild places."

Vail slapped Longarm on the shoulder. "No. No, my friend, you don't meet many like her. But if you're lucky in this life, there's always at least one, sometimes two."

As the men shook hands, Longarm said, "Ain't it the truth, Billy. Ain't it the God's truth."

On his way through the outer office to the Federal Building's bustling hallway, Henry, Billy Vail's trusted clerk, waved a small envelope and called out, "I have what might be an important communiqué for you, Marshal Long. Missive came just a few days after you left town for Trinidad. Lady admonished me to deliver the message into your hand, and your hand only. She said the note was of a personal nature. Right pretty thing she was. Damned beautiful as a matter of fact."

Longarm nodded, slipped the envelope into an inside pocket, then headed for the stairs that led to the first floor. He took the marble steps two at a time, then stopped outside the Federal Building's main entrance under the covered stone portico long enough to light a fresh cheroot.

He slid the note from his pocket and ran a finger under the waxed seal. His lips mouthed the carefully penned words on the half page of expensive linen paper. *How fortunate! My trip to Boston has been cancelled. Young men of the entire East Coast are completely safe. Need some of your* special attention. *Let me know when you get back to town. Geneva.* Longarm threw his head back and laughed out loud. "Women," he mumbled to himself. "Damned if I'll ever understand 'em."

Watch for

**LONGARM AND THE
GUNS OF FORT SABRE**

the 347th novel in the exciting LONGARM
series from Jove

Coming in October!

And don't miss

**LONGARM AND THE
GOLDEN EAGLE SHOOT-OUT**

Longarm Giant Edition 2007

Available from Jove in October!